D1196196

Books by Kathleen Pennell

Pony Investigator Series
The Case of the Missing Money
The Case of the Phantom Stallion
The Case of the Midnight Stranger
The Case of the Mysterious Circus
The Case of the Secret Passage
The Case of the Mirror Image

The Adventures In Time Series
The Door into Time
Rescued in Time
Lancelot Maddox Series
The Boy on the Bench
Ragtag Rescue
The Missing Agent
Plane Down

A Treadwell Mystery Series
The Face in the Water
The Man at the Ruins

A Treadwell
Mystery #1

THE FACE IN THE WATER

Kathleen Pennell

September 18, 1995

Estelle's life ended when her foot left the safety of the sidewalk.

It was dark. The car was dark, and it didn't stop.

The contract fulfilled, the driver only needed to make a phone call to the informant to collect his money.

John Calisto stumbled across the street and knelt by Estelle's side. Drops of blood slid down the side of her face. "Estelle," he whispered. "Estelle, I'm sorry."

Estelle's eyelids drew back halfway. She coughed. John eased his arm around her shoulder and lifted her to a half sitting position. "You promised," she whispered.

John nodded. "I won't forget."

Estelle's eyes closed.

Numbness enveloped him. When he heard the sound of sirens, John rose to his feet. On autopilot, he made his way home and climbed the steps to his second-floor apartment where he sat in the kitchen and stared into space until dawn.

As sunlight crept through the window, he drew a determined breath and made three phone calls.

"It's not who we thought it was," he said.

After completing the third call, John checked the suitcase he'd packed earlier, and added a large packet of cash to a box filled with carefully selected items.

Then he waited.

Chapter 1

At midnight, he checked the front and rear windows of his apartment. They were still there waiting for him. Two lights shone through windows of adjoining buildings. When those lights went out, they'd make their move.

He pressed the emergency number. When the call was answered, he said, "My grandmother lives in an apartment quite a distance from me. There are two men inside a car parked across the street from her apartment who have been watching her for the past three hours. She's quite anxious. Would you mind checking on it."

Within minutes, two police cars arrived. One pulled in back of the car across the street, another pulled in front. There were no sirens, but the lights created glaring reflections against the surrounding buildings.

John checked the rear window in his bedroom. They'd seen the swirling lights and had left. He picked up the box and his suitcase, made his way down the stairs and out the rear exit. His eyes maintained a steady watch on the surrounding area as he walked rapidly to his car. Once inside, he kept to the alleys and back streets until he reached the interstate, then headed north.

He'd carefully planned his escape route two months ago and stuck to that plan. He'd leave Cameron County and head north to Bedford County where he'd seek safety in a cabin. He pulled off the interstate and stayed in a nondescript motel with rooms the dimensions of an oversized closet. He hadn't slept the first night and was struggling to close his eyes when his phone buzzed.

The caller's number was unknown. John hesitated then answered it. "I know who killed Estelle." Immediately, the caller disconnected. John swung his legs over the side of the bed and rested his face in his hands. An hour later, it was the same caller with the same message: "I know who killed Estelle." The phone buzzed every hour, but John ceased to respond.

The following two nights were eerily quiet. John drove farther north on the interstate, pulling over at the next planned stop. At midnight, the caller returned. "Six o'clock tomorrow morning. Two miles east of the cabin along Muddy Creek."

Ominously, two thoughts surfaced. How did the caller know about the cabin? And would he survive the meeting?

John arrived at five thirty, parking his car next to a line of scraggly bushes with the front tires near the edge of Muddy Creek. He got out, leaving the door ajar, and peered through the shrubs, waiting for the caller to arrive. Thirty minutes later, a car stopped two hundred feet from where he stood.

"Pull over here," the caller said to his driver.

"There ain't nothin' here, Mister," his driver said.

"He's here. You just can't see him." The caller leaned forward and spoke to his driver. "Stay in the car. No matter what you hear, stay here."

"Okay, Mister." Afraid to reveal his true identify, "Mister" was the name the young driver had called his employer for over a year.

The man got out of the backseat and made his way along the road. When he rounded the bushes, the two men stared at each other through the meager pre-dawn light, measuring the other man's strength and resolve.

"Who killed Estelle?" John said.

A slow smile spread across the other man's face. "You did, John."

Voices rose. The caller, accustomed to settling arguments with his fists, threw the first punch. A struggled ensued. Having failed to gain the upper hand through brute force, the caller pulled out a gun with a silencer attached. One man survived; the other man lay with his face in the water.

The driver reached for the doorknob then remembered he was to wait in the car no matter what he heard. On the other side of the line of bushes, he heard a car start, put into gear, and move. He watched the end where the bushes met the road, but a car didn't appear. The only other direction the car could take was to move forward. But how could that be? There was nowhere to go but into the creek.

A man covered in blood rounded the bushes and staggered to the car. The gray horizon masked his identity. The man leaned against the car for a moment gasping for breath. With one last look over his shoulder, he opened the car door, and collapsed onto the backseat. "Take me to the cabin. I need to clean up," he said.

The driver parked the car beside a cabin. "Wait here," the man said. He made his way into the cabin where he attempted to wash off the blood that covered his clothes and hands. When he reappeared, his singular remark was, "We have to go back and clean up the mess."

The driver glanced repeatedly into his rearview mirror at the man whose eyes refused to meet his. The other man had to be dead, and he wondered how a dead body could be considered a "mess".

Ahead, they saw a car parked very near the spot they'd just left. "Back up around the bend," the man said. When their car was out of sight, the man got out. "Stay here."

The man walked along the edge of the road until he saw an older woman taking photos. From the protection of a tree, he waited and watched.

The sun was making a valiant effort to rise that September morning. Cynthia Treadwell, up since six, was attempting to capture the perfect angle for a shot of the red-headed woodpecker. The tricky little bird kept hopping about as if he'd forgotten trees were his natural habitat.

She knelt when the bird tilted his head to the rising sun. Perfect profile. She clicked several times in quick succession. Checking the shots on the display panel at the back of her camera, she smiled. It made leaving the house before tea and toast worthwhile.

Now, she could head back to her car with a clear conscience. Perhaps she'd find one or two bonus shots along the way. She was a tall, slender woman with a long, purposeful stride. Within moments, a gift stood not two hundred feet in the distance. A deer lowered his head to the creek with the sun sparkling all around him. His antlers reflected in the water.

She drew the camera to her eye, rotated the lens to get a closeup, and pressed down on the shutter button. Another smile. They were good shots. She studied the photos she'd just taken, then adjusted her bifocals. What was that shiny object protruding from behind the tree?

It appeared to be the front bumper of a car. Really! One positively did not park one's car partway into the creek. Sighing rather heavily, she marched forward. Pressing her palms together, she parted the shrubbery, resulting in one major and possibly two or three minor scratches.

Miss Treadwell broke through the tiresome shrubs on the passenger side of the car. The driver's side door was open, as was the car door behind it, and not a single person in sight. The silly fool. The car battery was probably dead by now. She worked her way around the back of the car and noticed tire marks behind the car. Evidently, the car had been parked farther back from the creek then, for some unfathomable reason, someone moved it to the edge of the water.

Moving beyond the back of the car, she stopped short.

When the brain can make no sense of what the eye sees, it freezes.

Miss Treadwell's brain stopped functioning as she gazed, open-mouthed, at the sight before her. Covering her mouth with a trembling hand, she stepped back then stepped back again.

Blood. There was blood on the steering wheel, on the open car doors and dark stains on the backseat. There was blood on the left front fender.

She inhaled sharply. Cautiously, she looked about, but didn't see or hear another human being. Her camera. Her camera could focus on objects impossible for the naked eye to see. She adjusted the lens to the highest level of magnification possible and slowly turned in a circle. Nothing. Was finding no one a relief or a worry?

A car. Blood. Yet there was no body.

She stepped cautiously forward, being sensible enough not to touch anything. Everything changed as she reached the front fender. She spied fingers then an entire arm. Stooping down, she saw the back of his head with his face resting in the water. The car had been moved forward to hide the body from anyone passing by.

Miss Treadwell sat down heavily at the edge of the creek, willing her lungs to draw in deep, sustaining breaths. Bile rose to her throat. She covered her mouth and swallowed hard several times, thankful for an empty stomach.

Her hand shifted to her forehead. Think! Yes, the police. The police must be called. She drew her phone out of her camera case. No signal. It was an isolated area. She'd have to leave the scene of the crime to call the police, but what if someone moved something or somehow contaminated the crime scene? It hadn't escaped her that she had done that very thing.

Armed with her resilient spirit, she drew the camera to her eye and shot photos of the body underneath the car close to the left front tire. To capture different angles, she stepped into the cold, shallow creek and stooped within a few feet of the body, then dropped back farther into the creek to gain perspective of the body relative to the shoreline.

Shivering from shock and the chill of the water, she stumbled out of the stream and began shooting the exterior and interior of the car as much as possible without touching anything. Moving to the rear of the vehicle, she took photos of the tire marks indicating the car had been moved at least ten feet closer to the creek to hide the body from anyone passing by on the road. Using a wide-angle lens, she shot verification photos three hundred sixty degrees until she returned to her original position.

With trembling fingers, she clicked through the display panel, inspecting every photo she'd taken. Dozens. She could make her way to the car, yet somehow it didn't seem right to leave that poor young man lying there with his face in the water. The side of his face was unlined and there was not a speck of gray in his dark hair. He was young and well-dressed. What was he doing out here in the middle of nowhere?

Had she missed anything? Probably. As she turned to leave, the angle of the rising sun exposed something hidden earlier. Miss Treadwell stepped closer and knelt beside the car. There, in the shadow of the front door, rested a pen. There was writing on it, but the dirt made it impossible to determine what it said.

At first, that's all she saw. The ground underneath where the pen rested was dry, so what held the dirt to the pen? She adjusted her bifocals. Even though it didn't surprise her, the visual representation came as a shock. The blood underneath the dirt acted as an adhesive. She swallowed hard. Obviously, blood was already on the pen when it hit the ground. Fresh blood. Did that young man drop it or did the pen belong to someone else? The one who killed him.

Miss Treadwell rose and checked the surrounding area. Subconsciously, her eyes were drawn to shadows and recesses. Except for the innocence of wildlife, it was deathly quiet. She turned to leave then remembered the evidence. She shot a close-up of the pen from several angles then stood back to include the driver's side door to give the location perspective. Now, she could leave.

Hampered by shock and low blood sugar, Miss Treadwell staggered to her car. Her head fell back against the headrest. It was then she realized she couldn't remember how to drive home. It was ridiculous. She'd been here dozens of times. She was positive. Or nearly positive. Her shaking hands beside the body of the dead man were nothing compared to her now trembling fingers as she attempted to insert the key into the ignition. The old engine refused to turn over, so she tried again, and again. On the third try, the car's engine roared to life.

Having accomplished that nearly insurmountable task, she headed in the direction the car faced. Her brain lacked the capacity to interpret what her eyes saw, because as soon as she pulled onto the road, a car slipped out from behind its cover and followed her. At first it followed from a distance, then slowly it moved closer until it was only a few feet away.

All she remembered of those next few minutes was leaving the safety of the road and someone opening her car door.

Chapter 2

Cynthia Treadwell was averse to raised voices. Yet someone insisted on shouting at her.

"Hey, lady! Ya awright?"

Miss Treadwell slowly opened her eyes. Leaning over her was a thoroughly disagreeable-looking young fellow. The word "seedy" came to mind. Unshaven, unkempt. His dark brown hair stood at unseemly angles, and his pasty white skin indicated a person unaccustomed to the outdoors. Sunglasses? The sun was barely above the horizon. "Please stop shaking my shoulder," she said in a slurred voice. "Who are you?"

The young man straightened. "Didn't mean ya no harm, ma'am. Jist tryin' ta help."

"That's very kind of you, but who are you?"

"Mike, ma'am. Everybody calls me Mike."

Her head throbbed. "What happened, Mike?"

"Well, ma'am. I was huntin', so ta speak, when I heared yer car hit that there tree. Came runnin' ta see if anybody was hurt. And that's how I found ya."

Through the fog, she wondered how one could be "huntin', so ta speak'? Moistening her lips, she struggled to make sense of everything. "Thank you, Mike. I'm very grateful." The images came back to her in bits and pieces until they formed enough of a picture that she reached for her phone. "I must—I must contact the police. Would you help me?"

"Police?" Mike looked warily at her, then over his shoulder. "Don't know about no police, ma'am. Why do ya want ta call 'em?"

As calmly as possible for someone suffering a slight concussion, she explained. "I think there's been a murder."

"Murder? What do you mean murder?"

"I found…." Miss Treadwell laid her head back and closed her eyes. Her mind, always sharp, had lost its capacity to reason. Yet one thing was abundantly clear. The edges of Mike's voice had smoothed out significantly. "I found a car parked partway in the creek. There was a dead body underneath the front bumper."

"Body you say. Have you called the police yet?"

His voice. Smooth, almost silky in tone. Miss Treadwell's head rolled back and forth. "No signal. Took photos. Dozens of them. On my camera."

"Is the camera on the floor the one you used?" the silky voice said.

"Yes."

"Does it have a memory card inside?"

"Memory card," Miss Treadwell murmured. Even in her jumbled state of mind, she perceived that question as an odd one. "Yes, memory card."

There was the faint whisper of voices. Soft, arguing whispers just

14

out of range.

In vain, she strained to open her eyes as she heard footsteps leave, then return what seemed like a moment later. More whispering, arguing voices. Her nose puckered as she smelled someone's stale breath on her face.

"You musta bumped yer head, ma'am," Mike said. "There's blood tricklin' down yer face. Let me jist dab it up for ya."

"Blood? I don't feel blood dripping on my face." Miss Treadwell slowly drew her hand to her forehead, but Mike gently pressed it down to her lap again.

"Don't want no blood smearin' all over them pretty little hands o' yers now, do we."

She felt the touch of cloth against her face as Mike held it against her skin. There was a faint odor, almost sweet. "What's that odor?" she said, struggling to turn her head.

"Nothin' to worry 'bout, ma'am. Just a little somethin' ta make everythin' we need ta do go a little bit easier. That's all."

"But what do you need…." Miss Treadwell had a vague sensation of someone rolling up her left sleeve, then felt a sharp jab.

The passenger car door opened. "Okay, I've got it. We can leave now," the silky voice said.

Rivers of perspiration slid down her face and her clothes felt damp. She opened her eyes, but everything was spinning, creating a queasy feeling in her stomach, so she squeezed them shut. She thought she heard the passenger side door close, then she knew no more.

After smoothing back the woman's hair and unrolling her left sleeve, Mike raced to catch up with the other man. "What'd ya give her, Mister?"

"Something to confuse her."

"Ya didn't give her no overdose, did ya? I mean nothin' more than ya had ta, right?"

"Probably not."

Mike grabbed the other man's arm and yanked him to a stop. "What do ya mean 'prob'ly not'? What'd ya give her and how much?"

"Look, we need time. We need time to clean up the mess and disappear for a while. You got that? You want her calling the police before we're through?"

Mike released the other man's arm, then trailed after him. "No. I don't want her callin' no police afore we take care of stuff."

"The only way to make sure she doesn't do that was to put her out for a while. Okay?"

"She'll be awright though?"

"Of course."

"You're not just sayin' that ta shut me up."

"Unless you want to spend the rest of your life behind bars, we'll do this my way." The man with the silky voice glanced at Mike with a raised eyebrow. "All right?"

Mike grunted by way of a response.

Having won that argument, he pressed on. "Give me your phone."

"What fer?" Mike said. "I might need ta call somebody."

"That's one of the reasons I want it."

"What's the other reason?" Mike said.

"The other reason? I need to keep in touch with certain people."

"What other people?" When no answer was forthcoming, Mike tilted his head and placed his hands on his hips. "What if I don't feel like givin' it ta ya?"

The man's right eyebrow rose. "You can give me your phone, or I can take your phone. Which is it?"

Slowly, Mike reached in his back pocket and handed over his phone. "Do I git it back?"

"Eventually," he said, then turned and continued on.

Mike watched the other man walk down the path. "We'll jist see 'bout that," he said softly.

Chapter 3

Cynthia Treadwell awoke to the sun's sweltering heat. Her clothes felt damp. Rivulets of perspiration slowly made their way down the sides of her face. Her eyelids quivered then drew back. She blinked and lifted an unsteady hand to lower the sun visor. Something had happened, but what? Isolated scenes slowly arose. The shock of discovering a hand, a face in the water.

Had she called the police? She couldn't remember. Fighting waves of nausea, she reached for the phone beside her on the seat. The phone rested next to the camera, where her purse should have been. Her purse had been moved to the floor. They'd been switched.

There was a hollowed-out cushion on the floor where she kept the camera, but her purse had taken its place. Not once had she forgotten, yet there the camera sat on the seat beside her. She was about to press the number for emergency service, when she noted it was eleven o'clock. Eleven? She'd been asleep for hours. She pressed the number and waited.

"Nine one one. What is your emergency?" came a brisk voice.

"This is Cynthia Treadwell. I'd—I'd like to report. I think there's been a murder."

The emergency dispatcher asked questions, but she had no idea how to respond. "Well, no, I'm really not quite sure where I am." She closed her eyes and laid her head back, realizing how inane her response must sound, then the voice on the phone brought her back. "Where am I? Somewhere in the northern part of the county. I'm fairly certain I'm near Muddy Creek," she said, looking out the side window. "Wait. There's a road marker. At least I believe it's a road marker." Her head throbbed. Her vision was blurred but she repeated what her unreliable eyesight captured. "Seven point five. I think that's what it says."

The emergency dispatcher assured her someone would be with her shortly.

"Shortly," she murmured. The phone slid out of her hand onto the floor, and she drifted back to unconsciousness.

The sound of an approaching car didn't awaken her. What brought her to consciousness was the opening and closing of the police car doors.

"Miss Treadwell," a worried voice said. "Are you all right?"

Miss Treadwell's lips curved slightly into a grateful smile. The policeman kneeling beside her car was one of the boys she raised at the boy's group home. "Ralph," she whispered.

"Don't worry. The ambulance is on its way. We'll have you out of here in no time."

"Ralph." She struggled to form the words. "There's been a murder. I took photos. Check the display panel in the back of my camera. You'll see everything."

"Murder? Just now? Did you witness it? Where did it happen?"

"Nothing like that. I was…." She moistened her lips before continuing. "I was shooting wildlife photos when I found the car and the body."

"Car and body?" Ralph said, drawing his hand over his sandy hair. What was she talking about? There hadn't been a murder in this neck of the woods in living memory, or was this the concussion talking? "Where did it happen?" he asked again.

Miss Treadwell pressed her hands against the side of her face as she struggled to remember. "A few miles back there, I think," she said uncertainly. "Although, I wonder. Perhaps it was in the opposite direction."

"I see. Okay. The ambulance will be here any second now. You'll be right as rain soon enough. We can talk about the murder later."

"Ralph! You must believe me! Take the camera back to the police station and examine the photos I took. You'll see that time is of the essence," she said, repeating a familiar quote routinely repeated throughout his life. Having delivered the lecture, her eyes closed, and her head fell back against the rest.

"Don't worry. I'll take care of it," Ralph replied softly. He nodded at Karl, the officer standing nearby, who opened the passenger-side door and, with gloved hands, carefully lifted the camera and carried it to the police car, where he placed it inside an evidence bag.

When the ambulance arrived, Cynthia Treadwell was transported to the hospital in Bedford. She was in the emergency room for a time, then admitted and transported to the third floor.

For the next twenty-four hours, she fought to remember. Her dreams were distressingly vivid. Blood dripped slowly down the steering wheel onto the floor of the car. The dream shifted to the man fighting to lift his head out of the water while someone else held him in place. She screamed but no one responded to her calls for help.

She struggled to remember exactly where she'd been, struggled to remember what she saw, struggled to remember what shots she'd taken. The only vivid daytime memory she had was that poor young man, dressed for work yet—he was covered in blood with his head face down in the water.

Chapter 4

September 23, 1995

The following day, Ralph took the elevator to the third floor of the hospital, walked into Room 324, and pulled up a chair beside her bed. "Do you remember anything about yesterday?"

Miss Treadwell recounted everything she could remember, which wasn't much and delivered in a jumbled fashion. "I got up early, before dawn, to see what wildlife shots I could capture," she began. "When I opened the display panel on the back of the camera, I was pleased with the shots I took. I noticed the tip of a car with its front wheels parked in the creek." She paused for Ralph's reaction. When there wasn't any, she continued. "You can see how odd that would be. A car parked with its front wheels in the creek."

"Yes, that's definitely odd. Do you remember anything else?"

She closed her eyes as vague scenes of that day floated through her mind but refused to take shape. "I remember working my way through those dreadfully scratchy bushes. You can see that by looking at my hands."

"I remember seeing them yesterday. Why didn't you walk around the bushes? Why go through them and risk an infection from the scratches?"

Why hadn't she walked around them? Normally she was so careful about things like that. "I really don't know," she said, softly. "It doesn't make sense, does it."

"Anything else you remember?"

Silence filled the room as she searched her memory banks. "There was a pen I almost missed. It was covered with dirt and hidden in the shadow of the open car door. The ground underneath the pen was dry, so I wondered how the dirt stuck to it. I saw traces of blood underneath it, Then I knew what held the dirt to the pen." Having recovered that lost memory, she sighed. "I don't know why I remember that particular detail but have forgotten so many others."

"You're suffering from shock and a concussion. It's only natural your memory is a little dodgy right now."

"You're right, of course. It has been quite a shock. I'm sure I'll be all right in a day or two. Just have to pull myself together." Her eyes slowly closed then reopened at the sound of Ralph's voice.

"You're tired. I'll stop by tomorrow on my way to the station."

"Thank you. I am a little tired."

Ralph kissed his mother lightly on her forehead and slipped quietly out of the room.

True to his word, Ralph stopped by on his way to the police station the following morning. "How are you, Miss Treadwell?"

"What is this with 'Miss Treadwell' all of a sudden?"

Ralph smiled. "Okay. How are you, Mom?"

"Worried. That's how I am. Now, tell me what you found on the camera."

Ralph walked to the window and peered unseeing at the parking lot. "Uh."

"Well?"

"We saw some birds. Quite a few birds. We saw a car but there was no dead body."

"No dead body?"

"No. There were wildlife photos and shots of a car but no dead body."

"I took dozens of photos before I left. I took shots of the car, the body, and that pen. You didn't see any of that?"

"No. We didn't see anything other than what I mentioned."

Miss Treadwell patted the side of her bed. "Come here and sit beside me."

As Ralph sat on the edge of her bed, he looked into her hazel eyes and waited.

"Do you believe what I told you yesterday?"

"Well, I've been thinking about it quite a lot since then."

"I want you to tell me the truth rather than what you think I want to hear. Understood?"

"Understood," Ralph said, drawing a deep, sustaining breath. "I think the concussion is worse than you realize. I don't know why you took photos of that car. But, somehow, you've created a story around it, and we can't find any evidence whatsoever to corroborate your claim there was a murder."

Miss Treadwell squeezed his hand, and said, "Thank you, dear. Thank you for being truthful with me. Now, I want to ask you a few questions. All right?"

"Okay."

"Did you find the car?"

"No."

"That means you have no idea where I took the photos."

"Oh, no. We know exactly where you took the photos. That was easy to find. We even saw car tracks where the car was parked when you took the photos. The front tires were right at the edge of the creek. Can't figure out for the life of me why anyone would park that close to the water. But that's all we found. By the time we got there, the car was gone. No car, no body, no pen, no nothing."

"No blood on the ground?"

"No, we didn't find blood anywhere."

"I see," Miss Treadwell said. "Yes, I see." She studied the tall, slender young man she'd raised since he was five years old. "I'm rather tired, Ralph. Would you run along so I can rest?"

"Oh, sure. I'll see you tomorrow," Ralph said. He was halfway across the room before he remembered. Smoothing back her silver-streaked hair, he tenderly kissed her forehead. "You get better real soon, Mom."

"I'll be fine, dear." After he closed the door, she reached for paper and pencil resting on her nightstand and began to write. She wrote everything she could remember from the time she left her house until the moment Ralph opened her car door the day she discovered the body.

Exhausted, she placed the notes inside her purse and closed her eyes.

Mike sharpened his knife, while the other man looked out the window. When Silky Voice slipped out of his chair and opened the door, Mike looked up. "Where ya goin', Mister?"

"Out. I won't be long."

"Ya be real careful, Mister."

"I'm always careful, Mike."

He drove through back streets and parked near a side entrance of Bedford Hospital. He took the stairs two at a time to the third floor. An air of confidence came easily to him, and no one questioned his right to be there. He walked down the hallway, checking each number until he arrived at Room 324. Quietly, he pressed through the door, allowing it to swing shut, then approached the bedside of the sleeping woman. He slid his hand inside the pocket of his white coat and withdrew a syringe. Her face was pale. An intelligent, peaceful face, but there was a quiet sense of strength and resilience about her. He gently touched her arm while he continued to study her. Slowly, he returned the syringe to his pocket and stepped back.

"Good morning, Doctor," said a voice directly behind him. "Is there anything I can do for you?"

"Good morning," Silky Voice said. "Just checking on a patient of a colleague. How is Miss Treadwell?"

"She's stable. A few problems with her memory," the nurse said as she prepared to take her patient's blood pressure. As the nurse wrapped the cuff around her patient's arm, Miss Treadwell stirred.

"Of course. I'm sure she'll be fine with rest and care."

The nurse smiled and nodded. "Yes. That's what we always hope for."

Miss Treadwell's eyes fluttered, so he stepped behind the nurse, blocking her view. "I'll leave you to it then," he said softly. Turning on his heel, he made his way back down the hall at the pace a doctor would assume. Once through the door leading to the stairway, he hurried down the steps and out the door, slowing to a walk to avoid drawing attention to himself. As he pulled out of the hospital parking lot, he made a call. "Has anyone contacted you?"

"Yes, but we didn't tell him anything."

"Good."

"Where are you?"

The man with the silky voice debated how much he should reveal. "Better not say."

"Understood," came the reply.

"Good. I'll check back later.

Chapter 5

September 24, 1995

Ralph stood outside his mother's room and stared at the floor. He allowed himself a moment of reflection before walking slowly to the elevator.

"Good morning."

Ralph looked up and immediately changed course. "Morning, Ms.—" he glanced at her name tag, then said, "Ms. Franklin. What can you tell me about Mother's condition?"

"Well, she's suffered a concussion. Not serious, but she's a little older, and that usually complicates everything."

"Has she mentioned a murder?"

The nurse dropped her eyes for a moment. "Yes. Yes, she has. She's spoken to most of us about it. It disturbs her quite a lot. We've given her something to quiet her nerves."

After spending fifteen minutes with his mother, Ralph decided the meds had fallen rather short of quieting her nerves. "Could she have imagined the murder, or do you think it may have actually happened?"

Ms. Franklin shook her head. "It's a bizarre story. I can't imagine it actually happened. But there's really no way of knowing. You're a police officer, aren't you?"

"Right."

"I read about it in the newspaper, and I shouldn't be asking, but have you found any evidence of a murder?"

Ralph shouldn't be discussing it either, but he made an exception in her case. "Nothing."

"I see. Well, the doctor will be here within the hour if you want to wait."

"Thanks, but I've got to report to work."

Ralph caught the elevator to the ground floor. He drove to the police station while a mantra replayed in his head: "What if, what if".

When he walked through the door, the officer on duty looked up. "Chief wants to see you."

"Right, thanks." Ralph tapped on the door and entered after he heard the Chief grunt his usual welcome.

Behind the desk sat a pudgy, pale, pugilistic sort of man. In the old days, a lit cigar would have hung out of the corner of his mouth. After some purists hung No Smoking signs all over the building, the cigar still hung out of the corner of his mouth. He just never lit it.

"So, what'd she say?"

"Still thinks it happened."

Chief Henderson nodded to a chair. "You tell her about that memory card business?"

"I told her."

"What'd she say about it?"

Ralph shrugged. "Still sticks to the same story."

"I see." The Chief shifted the cigar to the other side of his mouth. "I suppose she'll want to see me when she gets out."

"Don't know. The subject never came up."

"Well, you know how these older women are. Probably come crashing through that door the minute she gets out of the hospital."

"Actually, Miss Treadwell is quite intelligent and not given to exaggeration."

"Known her long, have you?"

"My parents were killed in a car crash when I was five. I had no relatives so ended up in a group home for boys. Miss Treadwell was our housemother. She raised me from then on. I think of her as my mother," Ralph said. "I don't discuss it here at work, so only a few people know about it."

"Ah, well. Stupid thing to say. Sorry, Ralph. I'm sure she's a fine woman."

"Yes, sir. She's a fine woman."

"Well, if she shows up, I'll talk to her."

"Thank you. She'll appreciate that."

"All right, that's all. Thanks for stopping by." Chief Henderson was about to return to his cluttered desk when he called Ralph back. "Look. You don't think there's a chance it actually happened, do you? You say your mother is an intelligent woman who doesn't exaggerate. Don't you think once her concussion gets better and she can think straight, she'll remember the murder never happened?"

Ralph stood with his hand on the door. "Chief, I lay awake nights thinking the very same thing. I've gone over the possibilities, but nothing makes sense."

"You see the problem, don't you?"

"Oh, yes, sir. I definitely see the problem. If a murder did take place, then some very smart people are covering it up. That's number one. Number two is, where does that place the only witness we have?"

Chief Henderson nodded. "In danger. That's where it places her."

Chapter 6

October 1, 1995

With no prior warning, Cynthia Treadwell pressed through the front door of the police station. She was pale and drawn but resolute. Her eyes swept the room, taking in every detail.

Officer Karl Farrell looked up in surprise.

"My name is Cynthia Treadwell, and I would like to speak to the person in charge."

"I know who you are, ma'am. I was on the scene the day of the accident."

"Oh, I'm so sorry. I don't remember your being there."

"No, ma'am. You were just barely conscious. How are you feeling?"

"A bit wobbly," Miss Treadwell said, laughing weakly. "But better than I was the day of the accident."

"You're up and about. That's a good sign," Officer Farrell said. "You'd like to see Chief Henderson?"

"Chief Henderson. I'd forgotten his name. Yes, I'd like to see him if he's not terribly busy."

"I'll see if he's free, ma'am."

"Thank you." Her eyes dropped to his badge. Officer Farrell. Yes, she remembered Ralph mentioning an officer named Karl Farrell.

Karl spoke softly into the phone, then led the way back to the last door in the hallway. He tapped, the Chief grunted, and the officer opened the door. "Miss Treadwell, sir."

Miss Treadwell studied the Chief with smiling eyes. She glanced at the placard on the wall behind him with his name emblazoned in bold letters. "It's so nice to meet you, Henry. I promise not to take up too much of your valuable time."

"Right, well…. Karl!"

"Yes, sir?"

"Tell Ralph to step in here right away."

"Yes, sir."

Without being invited, Miss Treadwell eased into the chair directly in front of the Chief's desk as her eyes swept the room. "You really could use a few pictures on the walls, Henry. Leave it to me. I know just the right person to handle it."

Chief Henderson was about to object when Ralph walked through the door. "Mom! You left your house."

"Yes, Ralph. I thought I'd have a little chat with Henry." Miss Treadwell smiled.

Ralph drew up a chair protectively close to his old housemother. "Are you feeling all right? You haven't been out of the hospital very

34

long."

Miss Treadwell placed her hand on Ralph's arm. "I've had the most trying morning, and with no breakfast. Would you trot across the street to that nice café? You know the one."

"Sure, I know the one you mean."

"I need my cup of tea. Actually, make it a pot of tea, and toast. Two pieces. Now, this is important. Ask for Teddy. You remember Teddy Clearfield, don't you?"

Ralph's brows slowly drew together. "Do I remember Teddy?"

"Yes, Teddy. He's the one with the dark ponytail and three rings in one ear. You know the one."

"I know who you mean," Ralph said, studying her face. "Don't worry. I'll talk to Teddy."

"Good. He knows how long to brew my tea and exactly how I like my toast."

"Yes, he knows exactly how you like it," Ralph said softly.

"Oh! Let me give you the money before you leave."

Ralph placed his hand over hers as she reached for her purse. "I'll take care of it," he said then glanced at the Chief. He'd already chewed his cigar halfway through. Ralph gave it another two minutes till he bit through the entire thing and it fell onto his lap. Wouldn't be the first time.

"Now, run along, dear. The sooner you leave, the sooner you'll get back."

"Right. The sooner I leave…." Ralph caught Chief Henderson's eye and was given a curt nod. Reluctantly, he slipped through the door, but not before giving his mother another studied glance.

"Now, just what can I do for you, Miss Treadwell," Chief Henderson said, with a voice reserved for the slow-witted.

Oh, Henry, please call me Cynthia," she said, with a smile reserved to charm the most disagreeable. She knew she'd won when the Chief took the cigar out of his mouth and placed it on the edge of his desk.

"Tell me about you and Ralph, Cynthia."

Miss Treadwell tilted her head as her mind drifted back over twenty years ago. "Well, you see, Henry, I had no one and Ralph had no one. We needed each other, you see. And there were two other boys in the same situation. I raised them, but when the oldest one turned seventeen, I had to make a decision. The state turns them out when they're eighteen." Her face took on a horrified look. "Eighteen with no family and nowhere to go. So, I left the boys' group home, bought a house large enough for the four of us, and took them with me."

"You bought a house for you and the three boys."

"Exactly," Miss Treadwell said, her smile still working its charm. "Now, Henry, I'm just wondering. I suspect I'm the very first person on the crime scene except for those dreadful people who murdered that poor man. I'm sure it hasn't escaped you there's a murderer out there somewhere."

"I understand what you're saying, Cynthia, but there's been no report of a missing person. Ralph has checked every day since you were in the hospital. It's not easy to just disappear without someone noticing it and usually reporting it," Chief Henderson said. "And beyond that, there's a problem with that, you know."

"Oh, yes, Ralph told me all about the situation with the camera. But you see, I have one advantage that no one else has."

"What's that, Cynthia?"

"I was there, and I saw the body."

Chapter 7

Oblivious to traffic, Ralph made his way across the street with his hands stuffed deeply into his pockets. He reached for the café door then stepped aside. He needed a plan before he faced Teddy. What did he intend to reveal and what tone of voice should he use? Didn't matter. Teddy would see through any deception. Always did.

Ralph walked to the far end of the café close to the kitchen door. He tapped his fingertips on the countertop while he waited for one of the servers to enter or leave the swinging doors. They'd notify Teddy he was here.

"Hey, Ralph. How's it going?"

"Teddy!" Ralph said, turning sideways. "Not bad. Well, not too bad."

"Is Mom worse?"

"No. Well, maybe. She's across the street talking to the Chief."

"What do you mean 'maybe'?" Teddy slid onto a counter stool and motioned for Ralph to do the same.

Ralph rested his chin on his cupped hands and closed his eyes.

"You need coffee, bud." Teddy walked around the counter, never taking his eyes off Ralph. He brewed a single cup of coffee then returned to his seat.

"Thanks." Ralph sipped his coffee, trying to decide how he was going to break the news.

"Is it the murder?" Teddy said. "Mom just can't let go of this murder idea of hers. Do they think it's the concussion?"

"I don't know. But think about it. Mom is not stupid. She has a logical mind. Has she ever been wrong about anything?"

Teddy inhaled deeply and exhaled slowly. "No. Never. Are you saying it could have happened even without a shred of evidence?"

"I don't know. I just don't know. The problem is the Chief wants us to drop it."

"Because there's nothing pointing to a murder on the camera's memory card?"

"That and we couldn't find anything at the scene where it was supposed to have taken place. We spent two full days scouring the area for something, but found absolutely no evidence," Ralph said, then remembered why he was there. "Mom wants tea, a pot of tea, and two pieces of toast."

"Right." Teddy put the water on to boil and pulled a teapot out of the cupboard.

While Teddy scooped Ceylon black tea into the teapot, Ralph carefully considered how to break the news to him.

Ralph wasn't the only one immersed in thought. Teddy observed and waited as he prepared the tea tray. "Ralph." When Ralph looked up, he said, "Just tell me."

"What do you mean?"

"Something's wrong. It's better to just say it."

"You really want to know?"

"I really want to know."

"Mom wanted you to make up her tea tray because you know how she likes it."

"Right. Made it hundreds of times."

"She told me to ask for you. Said something like, 'Ask for Teddy Clearfield. You remember Teddy, don't you?'."

Teddy stared at Ralph. "She forgot I'm one of her boys?"

Ralph's eyes drifted away. "No, no. It's not that. It's the concussion." He watched Teddy reconcile the fact that their former housemother had forgotten who he was.

Silently, Teddy placed two pieces of bread into the toaster and poured milk into a small pitcher. "Okay. Thanks for telling me. Where do we go from here?"

Ralph nodded, gratified that Teddy recognized it had nothing to do with her love for him. The important thing now was her recovery and safety. "We have to think of what she might do?"

"We know what she'll do," Teddy said emphatically. "She'll drive out to Muddy Creek and conduct her own investigation."

"I figured the same thing."

"We can't let her go alone, because there's always that incredibly remote possibility that she did see something."

"And run into the wrong people while she's there," Ralph said.

"And run into the wrong people while she's there."

Mike looked up as Silky Voice headed for the door. "Where ya goin', Mister?"

"Out. Won't be long."

"Goin' inta town agin?"

"No, taking a walk."

"Makin' a phone call and ya don't want me ta hear. Ain't that right?"

Silky Voice hesitated. "I won't be long." He walked a short distance then waited. When the boy didn't appear around the corner, he continued until he was well out of voice range and punched in a number. "What's happening?"

"A police officer stopped by several days ago, but you knew about that," the man said, his voice catching. "You did a good job of covering your tracks. I don't think they have any idea where you are."

"Good. I just hope nothing unforeseeable happens or that Mike decides to leave."

The man at the other end hesitated. "Where are you in case I need to get hold of you?"

Silky Voice placed his hand on his hip as he looked at the ground. "The guy's dead!"

"I know. I know."

"I might be next. It's just better if you don't know."

"Okay, I understand."

"I'd better get back."

"When will you call again?"

"Don't know. Soon." Silky Voice said, "I ditched my phone. This phone belongs to the kid. I think I should probably get rid of this one soon. Just to be on the safe side."

"Right. Don't want anyone tracing where you are."

"No. I'll call if I can."

Chapter 8

When Karl spotted Ralph crossing the street with the tea tray, he held the door open. "Your mother is in your office."

Ralph lifted a questioning eyebrow.

"Don't know. The Chief didn't raise his voice while she was in there, so it must have gone well. He even held the door open for her and wished her a nice day. No sign of a cigar hanging out of his mouth either. Smiled and called her Cynthia. At least it looked like a smile, sorta."

"That's a first."

"It's a first, all right."

Ralph quickened his steps down the hall. The door was ajar, so he shouldered through and pressed it shut. "How'd it go?"

"Fine. Only the tiniest bit tedious but otherwise quite nice."

Ralph set the tray on a small table. He sat down while she poured her first cup, studying her familiar movements as she sipped and looked out his singular window. "How are you feeling?"

Miss Treadwell's eyes smiled over her teacup. "A little sluggish. Like I need a good dose of cod liver oil. I'll be all right. Just need a day to collect myself, then we can get started."

Ralph knew it was coming but allowed himself to be drawn into the trap. "Get started with what?"

"The investigation," she said, pouring herself a second cup. "We positively cannot permit that poor man's murder to go unresolved."

Ralph started to protest, but his mother cut him off.

"Yes, I know, dear. But here's the difference. I saw that poor man dead with his face in the water and blood everywhere. You did not. Visuals are everything. Visuals are why people get dressed up to impress others. Now, how are you set for vacation time?"

"Well, I'll have to check."

His mother raised a knowing eyebrow.

Ralph swallowed a sigh. "Two weeks."

"Oh, plenty of time. And just think. If we solve the case before your vacation time is used up, you'll still have a few days left for an actual vacation."

Ralph leaned forward, placing his elbows on his knees. "What if we don't find anything? We've scoured that area and found nothing."

"I know, dear," Miss Treadwell said, using the look she gave the boys when she knew something they didn't. "But you didn't look in the right place."

"What do you mean? What 'right place'?"

"My car. Did anyone check my car?"

"Your car? Why would we check your car?" Ralph paused for a

moment. "You found something in your car, didn't you? What is it?"

"As soon as I've finished my tea and toast, we'll just walk outside and take a look, shall we?"

"You're parked outside?"

"Well, of course. I had no other means of getting here other than my car."

"I didn't see it out front when I walked to the café."

"No parking space in the front. I had to park around the corner."

"Do you really think you should be driving this soon after you were discharged from the hospital?"

"Well, the neighbor lady picked me up from the hospital. They're a bit stodgy about permitting patients to drive themselves home. You know how they can be." Miss Treadwell shuddered. "Have you ridden in Myrtle's car recently?"

"Can't remember the last time I did."

"Well, there's a reason for all the scrape marks on her tires. Do you know she cannot possibly park a car without subjecting those poor tires to the most appalling abuse? And have you noticed the dents in the fenders? I'm referring to the front as well as the rear fenders, of course."

"That bad?"

"You have no idea, Ralph. I gave myself a few days to rest at home, then decided driving in my somewhat weakened condition was certainly safer than Myrtle's driving."

"How old is she?" Ralph said, thinking both women must be close in age.

"Seventy if she's a day."

Ralph nodded. Nodding is always a safe answer.

Having finished her pot of tea and toast, Miss Treadwell stood and walked through the door Ralph held open for her. "Now, do you have one of those nice little evidence bags with you? And don't forget the gloves you wear to keep from touching the evidence."

"You did find something."

"I found something."

"What is it?"

"You'll see soon enough," she said evasively.

"Yer listenin' to somethin' agin and writin' agin," Mike said. "Whatcha listenin' to, Mister?"

"I'm listening to something the enemy said when he didn't know anyone was listening."

"Enemy? What kinda enemy?"

"The kind of enemy who wishes me dead."

Mike found reading difficult enough. Reading upside down was impossible. "What's all that there writin' 'bout?"

Silky Voice looked up, his pen poised over a notebook. "Details, Mike."

"Details? 'Bout what? What kinda details?"

"It's a diary of sorts."

"Diary? I seen diaries afore. People write stuff in them little books with locks on 'em so they're private like. So why ya usin' an ole notebook?"

Silky Voice leaned back in his chair. In spite of Mike's simple manner, he was observant. Perhaps a little too observant. "I have my reasons," he said with an edge to his voice. "Now, if you don't mind, I'd rather not discuss it."

Mike shrugged his shoulders. "Don't make no difference ta me. Jist askin'. That's all." He said, "How come ya won't tell me yer name?"

"Does it matter?"

"Course it matters! Anyhow, I don't like not callin' ya somethin'."

"Sorry, Mike. It's too dangerous for you to know my name. Too dangerous for me as well."

Mike blinked as he considered what the man sitting across the table from him just said. "Why is it too dangerous? Anyways, what ya doin' here anyhow? I don't mind or nothin'. Ya pay me good and stuff, but why don't ya go home?"

"What do you care?" Silky Voice sighed, laid down his pen, and leaned back in his chair. "Am I not paying you enough? Is that it?"

"No, sir. Yer payin' me jist fine. I jist wonder. That's all."

"All right, Mike. I'll tell you why I'm here. I'm trying to stay alive. That's what I'm doing here."

"Tryin' to stay alive? Who's tryin' ta kill ya? Ya says you got an enemy. So, who's your enemy? Ya afraid the police'll catch ya or somebody else?"

Silky Voice stared out the window at the woods that surrounded the cabin. There was a narrow path beside the cabin that ran another half mile deeper into the woods. The main road was a half mile in the opposite direction. There was a small rest stop next to the main road where the path leading to the cabin began, but whoever created the path did an excellent job of hiding it from the curious.

"Both. Right now, I'm afraid of both. I'm afraid of what I don't know. That's why I'm hiding." With that, Silky Voice continued writing in his spiral notebook.

Mike sharpened his pocketknife, checked it for sharpness, and continued to carve the piece of wood that would eventually evolve into a dove.

Chapter 9

Ralph studied the dent on the right side of the car below the trunk. "I'd forgotten about this. I spotted it the day of your accident, but it completely slipped my mind. Do you remember if the dent was there before the accident?" When his mother appeared puzzled, he said, "I'm talking about the morning you blacked out after taking the photos."

"Blacked out?" Miss Treadwell murmured. "I blacked out and ran into the tree. Well, I—I don't know," she said vaguely. "I'm sure I would have felt it had I been in the car."

"It's conceivable someone ran into you and that's what caused the accident. They could have left the scene of the accident without reporting it. Although, I assumed you fell asleep, took your foot off the accelerator, and drifted into that tree."

His mother was at a complete loss as she stood beside Ralph, sharing the mystery of the dent. This was her first day driving the car. The door to the garage opened on the driver's side, so she hadn't seen the back of the car since before the accident. There was something about that dent, but she couldn't quite put her finger on it—a memory pressed so far back in her mind it refused to come to the forefront.

Leaving that concern behind, Ralph said, "Okay. Tell me what I'm supposed to look for and where it is."

Miss Treadwell led the way to the driver's side door then reached for the handle, but Ralph placed a gentle hand on her arm.

"Let me put on my glove. I realize you've already touched the handle, but let's just go by the book."

"Of course, I should have thought of that."

Ralph slipped on his gloves, opened the car door then raised an eyebrow.

"Right there. Do you see the tissue? I never use tissues, so someone else dropped it, it slid down the driver's side seat, and got lodged. I only noticed it after I parked the car and turned around to close the door."

"It's not yours then?"

"No, I have at least a dozen linen handkerchiefs. My mother embroidered the edges of the handkerchiefs years ago while she was still alive. You must have seen them."

"You're right. I've seen them. I wonder if the tissue belongs to Karl. He drove the car to your house."

"Oh, I never thought of that. It very well may be."

"Karl's at the front desk right now. I'll ask him as soon as we get this bagged." Ralph placed the tissue inside the evidence bag, wrote pertinent information on it, and sealed it.

"What are you going to do with the tissue?"

"I'll check with Karl first. If it's not his, I'll take it to the lab. I know someone there, so the turnaround time should be short unless Sam's working on something that's critical. We'll drop it off on our way to Muddy Creek. I want to leave your car here. Depending on what's found on the tissue, we'll do a more thorough search of your car for further evidence."

"Why not do a more thorough check on the car now?"

"Chief Henderson called off the investigation, so I need to think about people who owe me favors or people I can trust to help us."

"Ralph, this has nothing to do with the investigation, but my car would barely start this morning. I was terribly worried I might have to depend on Myrtle to drive me here."

Ralph suppressed a smile. "What's wrong with your car?"

"I had to turn the ignition three times before it finally started. Once it started, it was fine, but I must say I doubt very much if I could trust it in an emergency. I know it's an old car, but I've grown rather used to it and don't really want another one."

"When is the last time you had a tune-up?"

"Oh, dear. Well, I have no idea. You know how I am with cars, Ralph. I don't want to worry about them. I just want them to work," Miss Treadwell said, "Now, you know I'm very capable in most ways, but I just cannot be bothered with tune-ups and computers that don't work the way they should."

"Is your computer giving you a problem?"

"Not yet, but I'm afraid I'm rather fatalistic when it comes to cars and technology."

"Would you like me to make an appointment at the garage, or do you want to take care of it yourself?"

"You're much too busy, Ralph. I'll take care of it."

Having settled the troublesome details about the car, they walked back to the station.

As they neared the door, Miss Treadwell said, "Oh, I nearly forgot. Is my camera here?"

"Thanks for reminding me. It's in my office. We'll pick it up after we check with Karl."

Karl studied the evidence bag, "No, it's not mine. I always carry a small packet of tissues in my pocket, but I definitely didn't use a tissue while I was driving the car."

Miss Treadwell waited at the front of the station while Ralph picked up the camera. "My car doesn't seem to have suffered much damage," she said to the top of Karl's head.

"Only a slight dent in the front fender. You must have passed out and taken your foot off the gas pedal, so it just drifted off the road. Well, and there was a larger dent in the back, too. Someone must have run into you."

"That's what Ralph said, Karl. But I don't remember someone running into me. And with the size of the dent, I think I would have felt it."

"Oh, yes, ma'am. You'd definitely feel a bump that size," Karl said. "You sure were lucky, ma'am."

"Yes, very fortunate indeed. Another was not quite as fortunate that day."

"How's that?"

"The man who was murdered."

"Oh, well. We're not too sure about that, ma'am. The problem is we didn't find any evidence."

"Yes. Chief Henderson and Ralph have been through that with me."

Miss Treadwell's camera rested on her lap as they drove to the lab where the tissue would be analyzed. Afterwards, she was never quite sure what prompted her to view the photos on the display panel in the back. Her first impulse was that her son had picked up the wrong camera. She inspected the camera closely. No, it was definitely her camera. She studied Ralph for a moment, not quite sure what to say.

Feeling her eyes on him, Ralph said, "What is it?"

"These aren't the photos I took."

Chapter 10

Ralph took his eyes off the road long enough to glance at the camera. "You sure?"

"Positive. There are photos of birds. But none of them are the red-headed woodpecker and they're all resting on the limbs of trees, not on the ground. I took several shots of a deer in the stream. They're not here either. They've been erased along with nearly everything else."

"There's half a dozen shots of the passenger side of a car."

"Yes, but it's the wrong car! And it's parked in another spot. That's not the area I photographed. I have no idea where these photos were taken." Miss Treadwell felt her anxiety rising. "I took dozens of shots. I took photos from every conceivable position. I took shots of the body from as many angles as I could. I even waded into the stream, so you'd have some idea how the car was positioned. They've all been erased!"

"Aren't the photos numbered? Wouldn't you see that dozens of photos have been erased because the sequence of the numbers is off?"

"It doesn't work that way." She drew a deep breath. "Say I take forty photos and they're numbered from one to forty. Then suppose I erase numbers eight and ten. Are you with me so far?"

"I get it. You've just erased photos eight and ten."

"Right. When photos are erased, the numbers are adjusted, so it appears I took thirty-eight photos rather than forty. No one would know any photos had been erased. They're still sequential." Miss Treadwell pressed her hand against her forehead. "I read somewhere that there's a way to recover erased photos. I don't know anything about it, because I'm very careful which photos I erase, so I haven't looked into it yet."

"Recover them? We'll ask Sam when we get to the lab."

Ralph pulled into the parking lot of a gray building indistinguishable from any of the other nondescript buildings in the entire block. He held the front door open for his mother, then walked up to the counter and waited for Paul to finish his phone call. When the call was completed, the man looked up with raised eyebrows.

"Hi, Ralph. What can I do for you?"

"Hi, Paul. Is Sam in?"

"Sure. Give me a sec to find out what's happening in the back."

Suddenly exhausted, Miss Treadwell leaned against the counter, hoping Ralph wouldn't notice. He appeared oddly out of sorts. He stared at the door the man just walked through while drumming his fingertips on the countertop. Thirty seconds later, she understood. Through the door walked an attractive young woman wearing a shy smile.

Sam was above medium height and slender. There was an air of understated confidence about the woman. She was capable, knew it, but didn't feel compelled to impress you with it. "Hi, Ralph."

"Hi, Sam."

Miss Treadwell studied the young man she claimed as a son. She'd never seen that expression on his face. It rather mirrored the expression on the young woman's face as well.

"Would you have time to take a look at this tissue?" Ralph said.

"Where did you find it?" Sam said.

"It was in Miss Treadwell's car, so I'd like to know whatever you find out about it."

"Is this a priority?"

"Well, not officially," Ralph said.

"I understand. I'll take care of it for you this morning." Sam smiled at the older woman. "You're Miss Treadwell?"

"Oh, sorry, this is my, uh...."

"I'm Ralph's mother." The two women grinned at each other.

"Ralph has mentioned you so many times, so it's very nice to meet you," Sam said.

Ralph stood to the side wearing a repressed grin as the two women exchanged information about where they lived progressing to the names of Sam's pets.

"Sam, I'm curious about something," Miss Treadwell said, placing her camera on the counter. "If photos are erased from the memory card, is there any way to retrieve them?"

"Yes. We have equipment here in the lab to retrieve photos that have been erased." Sam said, "Have photos been erased that you want retrieved?"

"Well, yes. I don't know whether Ralph told you about the body I found and the accident I had afterwards."

Sam glanced at Ralph. "Yes, he mentioned something about it," she said, without further comment.

"The problem is I took dozens of photos of the body and surrounding area, but they've all been erased. I have no idea how it happened. If they can be retrieved, that would be the evidence we need to move forward with the case."

It didn't escape Sam's notice that Miss Treadwell used the words "we" and "case" when referring to the obscure mystery. "Of course, there's no guarantee, but I'll see what I can do about retrieving the lost photos from your memory card," Sam said, then turned to Ralph. "Look, the retrieving process won't take long. Would you like to wait a few minutes while I work on it?"

"Sounds good," Ralph said. "Thanks, Sam."

Sam slipped on a pair of evidence gloves before removing the memory card from the camera. She picked up the evidence bag holding the tissue and headed through the door into the lab. After the door closed, Ralph said, "Why don't we sit down."

They sat side by side. Ralph rested his ankle over his knee. Within fifteen seconds, he swapped the other ankle for the opposite knee. His eyes swept across the room, then swept again.

"Are you worried, dear?"

Ralph looked down at his mother with raised brows. "Worried? About what?"

"Well, worried about anything."

"I'm worried about everything right now."

She drew her hand through her son's elbow. "Tell me. Or would you rather not?"

Ralph rested his head back against the wall. "I'm worried about you."

"Why?"

"I'm worried about your concussion. I'm worried that the murder, which seems so real to you, never happened. On the other hand, I'm worried you may be right about the murder. Maybe it did happen, which means you may be in danger."

Miss Treadwell patted his arm. "I know. Actually, I'm a little worried about all those things, too."

Ralph covered her hand with his larger one. And that's how they remained until the door opened.

Sam walked through the door, her eyes averted from the two in the corner.

Averted eyes were a bad sign. Miss Treadwell knew this from her long experience raising youngsters at the group home for boys.

Sam's eyes remained averted as they approached the counter.

"I'm sorry, but I couldn't find any sign of erased photos. I ran through them twice and found nothing."

"Nothing," Miss Treadwell murmured. Her first thought was, had she imagined it? Did it really happen or was the entire memory a product of her concussion?

"But I'm wondering about something," Sam said, tentatively.

"What is it?"

"How long have you had this memory card?"

"How long? Well, let me think. About two years. Perhaps more."

"I see." Sam's face was a study in confusion. There was a battle ensuing in her mind.

"What is it, Sam?" Ralph said. "Just tell us. Even if it sounds unbelievable, just tell us."

"I looked at the memory card under magnification. I could see the manufacturer's mark on it. They only started manufacturing this type of memory card in the last six months."

It took Ralph exactly two seconds to connect the dots. "That's not Mom's memory card. Someone took her memory card out, replaced it with another one, and shot all those photos to mislead us."

Sam nodded. "Exactly."

Chapter 11

Miss Treadwell felt vindicated. She also felt light-headed. "I think I'd better sit down," she said weakly, taking Ralph's arm.

Sam gently grasped her other arm and they led her to a chair. They sat on opposite sides, watching her closely.

"Would you like water?" When there was hesitation, Sam said, "Tea or coffee?"

"I've already had my tea, but I do feel as though I could really use another cup."

"Of course. I'll just be a few minutes."

Ralph massaged his mother's hand. "This changes everything. You realize that, don't you?"

"I do. I do realize it." Miss Treadwell looked up and made a remarkable effort to smile. It was a bit lopsided, but Ralph was hopeful since she made the effort. She leaned her head against the wall and closed her eyes. Tea. She heard the rattle of the teacup on its saucer.

"This should help," Sam said. "Can you handle holding it?"

"When it comes to tea, I could be half dead and still hold my cup and saucer. Thank you so much, Sam." She took two sips in quick succession, then smiled gratefully. "This is as good as the tea one of my boys brews. Teddy. Do you know him? He owns the café across the street from the police station."

"Oh, yes. I know Teddy," Sam said, giving a quick glance at Ralph, whose face mirrored her own sense of relief mixed with confusion. Only an hour earlier, Ralph had given her a quick call explaining his mother seemed unaware that Ralph and Teddy grew up together and were best friends. "I didn't realize Teddy was one of your boys," she said, in a fishing sort of way.

"Oh, yes. Teddy is close to Ralph's age. You're twenty-seven?" When Ralph nodded, she continued. "Teddy's birthday falls exactly one month after Ralph's, but he's a year older, you see. The boys were inseparable growing up. Still are, aren't you, dear?"

Ralph nodded, trying to hide the relief he felt. But why had she led him to believe she didn't know Teddy? Or was it the lingering effects of the concussion?

"Then, of course, there's Bobby. He moved rather far away. California. We don't see too much of Bobby. But he calls and sends little packages for birthdays and holidays. Very thoughtful." Miss Treadwell handed the empty cup and saucer to Sam, then stood on firmer legs. "Thank you again, Sam. The tea was delicious and restored me to normal. Well, as normal as can be expected under the circumstances."

Shouldering her purse, she turned to face Ralph. "Best get started. Can't waste valuable time." She made her way slowly to the door while Ralph and Sam exchanged a few clipped whispers.

Ralph pulled out of the parking lot, then gave Teddy a quick call to bring him up to date.

"So, you're headed out to Muddy Creek now to see if Mom can find the spot," Teddy said.

"We'll be there in about twenty minutes. I thought you'd want to know."

"You're right. Thanks for calling me. Everything has changed now."

"I know. Everything has changed. I'll see you later, Teddy." His mother's face was drawn. How hard should he press her? "Why don't I show you where those photos were taken?"

"Yes, I'd like to see it."

"Do you remember where you took the photos that morning? I mean where you found the car with the body underneath it?"

"I'll never forget what the area looked like, but I'm trying to remember how I got there or where I parked my car while I took the photos. I've spent over a week writing down everything I could remember, but there are so many gaps in my memory."

"Do you have the notes with you?"

"Right here," Miss Treadwell said, tapping her oversized purse.

"Good. We'll take a look at them when we get back to the station."

Twenty minutes later, Ralph pulled his car onto a grassy area beside Muddy Creek. "This is where the photos on the memory card were taken."

"Yes. I can see that."

Ralph placed his arm on top of the steering wheel as he considered his mother's level of fatigue. "Are you up to taking a quick look around before we go any farther? I realize this doesn't look familiar to you, but there's always the possibility something you see may jog your memory. There's also the possibility that you took photos in two separate locations and only remember one of them."

"Yes, I see your point." Miss Treadwell stood beside the car, hanging onto it while her head cleared.

"You sure you're up to this?"

"I'll be all right. Just a bit lazy." Her eyes drifted over the area, looking for something that might be vaguely familiar.

"Is there anything that makes you think you may have been here before?"

"I don't think so. Nothing looks familiar. Areas along a creek can look very much the same, but I just don't recognize anything I'm looking at."

When they were within twenty feet of the creek's edge, Ralph pointed to tire tracks. "We never doubted that you were the one who took the photos. The ground has hardened since that day, so you can still see where the car in the photo was parked. But the day we came to investigate, there was absolutely nothing suspicious about it. We figured someone went fishing or hiking. By the time we arrived, they'd packed up and left.

"Now you're convinced those photos aren't mine."

"Right. Those photos are not yours."

"So, no one actually saw the car because someone had moved it by the time you and the other police officers got here," Miss Treadwell murmured.

"Right. It was gone by the time we got here. When we looked at the photos, we recognized where it was taken because the camera picked up the bend in the creek. When we saw the tire marks, we figured we found the spot that was in the photos."

"But there are photos of a car on that memory card. Won't that help identify it?"

"No," Ralph said. "The problem is it's a popular make of car. There are thousands of them. With no shots of the license plate number or any other distinguishing features, it's impossible to trace it."

"Ralph, it's terribly upsetting that a body has just been dumped somewhere. But what about the people who murdered him? We have no idea who they are. They could be anyone or anywhere."

"I know, Mom. We've lost valuable time because they're clever. They switched the digital card in your camera and took other photos. They delayed the investigation long enough that even when we find the right location, all the evidence has probably been destroyed."

Ten minutes later, they were making their way back to the car when Ralph's phone vibrated. He looked at the caller, smiled and answered, "Sam?" His smile disappeared almost instantly. "You sure? But this means…" he said, glancing nervously at his mother who, in turn, studied him with growing anxiety. "Would you do me a favor, Sam? Would you ask some of the lab people to go over Mom's car with a fine-tooth comb? Right. Oh, Sam. There's a dent on the right rear side of the car. Ask them to look into that, too. Paint particles from another car. You know what to look for." He listened for a few seconds. "It's never locked. Well, I may have locked it out of habit. Just a second." He drew the phone away from his face. "I didn't lock your car, did I?"

"No, you didn't lock it."

"We'll head back to town right now and talk with the Chief. I know he'll authorize us to open the case again." Ralph ended the call. "Come on, Mom. We need to head back to the station." He placed a protective arm around her, but she drew back and turned to face him.

"Ralph," she said, grasping both his arms. "What did Sam tell you?"

Ralph bit his lower lip as he gazed over her head. "It's, uh, it's serious, Mom."

"Just tell me. I know Sam called to give you the test results on that tissue. What did she find?"

"She found traces of Diethyl Ether on the tissue."

Chapter 12

It took Miss Treadwell several seconds to mentally unpack what Ralph had said. "Ether. Do you mean ether as in something that puts people to sleep? Is that the kind of ether she found?"

"It's that kind of ether. Primitive, but it works."

They continued to make their way to the car as both silently contemplated Sam's call. "Ralph?"

When she failed to continue, Ralph said, "What is it?" Still, there was silence. "Mom, tell me what you're worried about."

"I don't know much about medicine, but it seems to me that ether doesn't keep someone asleep very long. Do you follow me?"

"I understand. Ether is short-term."

"If that's the case, how could I have slept so long? I must have slept for at least four hours."

"Four hours?" Ralph murmured. "It may have been the concussion."

"I understand what you're saying, but I don't think that was it."

"What do you mean?"

Miss Treadwell drew on her formidable resources to maintain equilibrium. "There were things I remembered as soon as I woke up that day. I remembered enough to call the police. I remembered there'd been a murder. Other things have come back to me in bits and pieces."

"You've suffered a concussion as well as had a tremendous shock, so your memory is a little shaky."

"Yes, it's still a bit shaky. Something happened that day," Miss Treadwell began. "It seems so much like a dream, but I feel certain it actually did happen. I remember someone pressing a piece of cloth, perhaps that tissue, to my forehead because he said I was bleeding.

"But I wasn't bleeding. Had I been bleeding, someone at the hospital would have noticed and tended to it. The cut wouldn't have healed so quickly that it disappeared two days later when I looked in the mirror. So, he must have used that as an excuse to place the tissue close to my nose. I felt drowsy. Then I had the sensation that someone was rolling up my sleeve." She stopped as they reached the car. Her eyes blinked in rapid succession.

"What happened next? Do you remember?"

Miss Treadwell's eyes stopped blinking and her head tilted back to look at her son. "A sharp jab. I felt a sharp jab in my left arm. Right about here," she said, touching the upper part of her left arm. "Then, the last thing I remember was the opposite door opening and closing."

Unable to speak, Ralph put his arms around his mother and drew her close.

"Well, this changes things a bit, doesn't it?"

"Yes, this changes everything, Mom," Ralph said, controlling his voice with a great deal of effort. "Most likely you'll remember other things as time goes by. Keep your notepad handy and write down whatever comes to mind, no matter how trivial."

"I will."

Ralph drew back and studied his mother's face. "Are you all right?"

"I think so. That fleeting memory gave me pause."

"I'm sure it did."

"Ralph, something else just came to me."

"What is it?"

"A man's voice," she whispered. "And another voice. A different man's voice."

"Two separate men. Do you remember anything about either of them?"

Miss Treadwell closed her eyes tightly. "One of the men. He was young. At least my impression was of someone young. He had dark hair. It stood out at strange angles. He said, 'I was hunting'. No, it wasn't that. He said, 'I was huntin', so to speak'." She turned to Ralph, whose eyes studied her intently. "That seemed to be an odd way to put it. 'Huntin', so to speak'. How can one hunt, so to speak? You're either hunting or you're not hunting."

"Yes. 'So to speak' is a very odd way to put it."

"His name."

Ralph stared at his mother, only daring to hope.

"Mike."

Chapter 13

"Mike?" Ralph said. "His name was Mike?"

"Someone opened my car door. I must have asked who he was because he said his name was Mike."

"Is he the one you thought was young?"

"Yes. I had the impression he was very young."

"Can you remember anything else about him? What was his approximate height, weight, coloring, anything like that?"

"Frame of reference," Miss Treadwell murmured. "You and Teddy have both stooped beside my open car door to talk to me. Teddy is about four inches shorter than you. Wouldn't you say?"

"Right. I'm six two; Teddy is about five ten."

"Well, then Mike is about five ten, because as he stooped, his head was about the same height as Teddy's is when he's in the same position."

In spite of the tension he felt, Ralph smiled. "You know something? You never fail to amaze me."

"Thank you, dear. That was a lovely thing to say."

Ralph allowed his mother a moment to bask in the distraction of his compliment, then said, "Anything else?"

Miss Treadwell closed her eyes again as she replayed that scene. "Dark hair. I don't remember the color of his eyes. He may have worn sunglasses, which is odd since it was so early in the morning. Very thin. I remember he was very thin because his t-shirt was baggy. It just hung on him like he'd lost weight or was wearing someone else's shirt. When he lifted his arm to place the cloth on my forehead, I noticed there wasn't much flesh on it. Age. His skin was smooth, unlined. When he spoke, his voice reminded me of someone who is youngish rather than older," she said, opening her eyes. "If you know what I mean."

"I know what you mean. A person's voice changes with age."

"I'm afraid that's all I can remember now."

"About five ten, dark hair, very thin with a young-sounding voice is a lot of information. A week ago, you didn't remember any of that. More may come to you as your mind clears."

"Yes. More may come."

"Mom, I need to call the Chief. There's enough evidence to reopen the case, but I need his permission."

"Yes, of course. Shall we go back to the station?"

"Well, I thought about that," Ralph began as he stroked his chin. "The problem is, now that we've eliminated this as a possible crime scene, I'd like to find the spot where you took the photos and discovered the car. But only if you're up to it."

Miss Treadwell was fairly trembling with fatigue. Even so, she rallied and said, "Of course I'm up to it. That is the scene of the crime and we need to find it as soon as possible."

"Okay, I'll call the Chief." Ralph lifted an eyebrow as he looked at his mother. "I don't know what he's going to say when I tell him I personally authorized lab work on that tissue without discussing it with him."

"Yes. I see what you mean. Would you like me to talk to Henry? I'm sure I can reason with him."

Ralph studied his shoes until he got his face under control. "Don't worry, Mom. I think I can handle it." For several minutes, he gave a step-by-step account of the past three hours. Ralph remained silent as Chief responded, then he said, "Okay, Chief. Here she is." He handed his mother the phone and whispered, "He wants to talk to you."

"Henry? How are you?"

"I'm fine, Cynthia. I hope Ralph isn't tiring you out too much."

"Oh, no, Henry. He's taking great care of me. It's amazing what he's discovered in such a short time."

"It's an incredible story, Cynthia." Chief Henderson paused, and for the first time in his entire police career said, "We owe you an apology, Cynthia. I owe you an apology. I shouldn't have closed the case until after you recovered and I'd spoken to you."

"I do understand, Henry," Miss Treadwell said graciously. "I'm sure it's terribly difficult to continue an investigation without a shred of evidence. But now we have that, so it's a question of who murdered that poor man and finding the body and car."

"Quite right," Chief Henderson said.

"And the pen. Did I mention the pen? That's a very critical piece of evidence, Henry."

"Yes. The pen is a crucial piece of evidence," Chief Henderson said. "Cynthia, I'd like to speak to Ralph again. Would you put him on the phone?

"Of course, Henry. It was lovely chatting with you," Miss Treadwell said, the phrase she used with everyone.

"Look, Ralph you'll need to drive along the river until Cynthia can identify where it happened. I'm sure you've already planned to do that. The sooner the better."

"Yes, sir. We'll leave as soon as we're finished here," Ralph said. "If she's up to it."

"Naturally; she just got out of the hospital not long ago. We need the information ASAP, but only take it as far as she is able and no further."

"Right, Chief. We'll take it easy."

"Anything else?"

"Chief," Ralph began. "I'd like authorization to have the tissue sample tested for DNA."

"Yes, yes, of course," Chief Henderson said. "Top priority. Get hold of the lab as soon as we hang up. Okay?"

"Thanks, Chief."

"I'm sure I'll hear back from you as soon as you find anything," Chief Henderson said, with a touch of dryness in his voice.

"Yes, sir," Ralph said, rather sheepishly. "I'll report back what I find."

"I should hope so. As soon as Cynthia identifies where it happened, call in the exact location and I'll send people out to collect whatever evidence they can find. It's been long enough now, so I'm not sure what's left."

"Yes, sir. As soon as we identify the location, I'll call in."

"Good," Chief Henderson said, then ended the call.

"Look, Mom. Are you sure you're up to driving along the creek to see if you can identify where it happened?"

"Yes, I'm up to it," his mother said, drawing on strength she didn't know she possessed. "There won't be anything to investigate until I find where it happened."

Ralph drove slowly down the road as his mother leaned forward, looking for something familiar.

"It all looks so much alike."

"I know. It's a tough call deciding where the exact spot is when the scenery doesn't vary that much."

"I'll look for that line of bushes. I can only suppose the bushes stretched out quite a length and I didn't want to take the time to walk around them." They drove another half mile, then she pointed directly ahead. "There! I think that's the place."

Ralph parked well beyond the spot, not wanting to contaminate the scene beyond the contamination it had already undergone. He sat for a moment composing his words carefully. "Mom, people often have flashbacks when they return to identify certain aspects of the scene of a crime where they were victimized or suffered trauma. This may be tough for you, so let me know when you need to leave. Agreed?"

Miss Treadwell moistened her lips and nodded. "Agreed."

"We need to make fairly certain this is the spot before I call the Chief."

"We can't have people swarming about wasting their time when it's the wrong place."

His mother appeared pale and drawn but resolute. Should he take her arm? Perhaps not yet.

They walked slowly to the far side of the bushes, and carefully approached so as not to disturb any evidence that may still exist. Ahead, they saw marks on the ground where a car had been parked.

Miss Treadwell stepped back, then stepped back again as she covered her mouth with her hand. Her mind drifted back to that morning when she stood in this very spot, trying to make sense of the horror that unfolded before her. "There," she said, pointing with a trembling hand. "The pen was buried beside the open door. And the body was underneath the car with his face in the water."

Chapter 14

Ralph gently drew his mother away from the horror she'd witnessed. He settled her in the car and waited a moment while she laid her head back and closed her eyes. "Are you all right?"

"I'm a little shaky," Miss Treadwell said, her voice a testimony to her emotional state. "I just need to rest a minute."

"I have to call the Chief and give him the location. And I want to call Sam and ask her to send that tissue to a lab and have it tested for DNA."

"Yes. You need to call Henry and Sam. I'll just rest while you do that."

Ralph stepped outside of earshot to make his first call. "Chief? She found it."

"Okay," Chief said. "I'll have a team out there as soon as possible. Sit tight, Ralph. Won't be long."

"Right, thanks, Chief."

Before he punched in Sam's number, he stepped back to the car.

"How are you doing, Mom?"

"Better." Miss Treadwell put on a brave if pale face. "Is Henry sending a team?"

"They'll be here in a few minutes."

"How's Sam?"

"I'm just going to call her."

"She works too hard."

Ralph nodded. They all worked too hard. "Sam? Look, Chief Henderson authorized a DNA sample. Can you send that tissue sample off today? Good. Is the turnaround time still about two weeks on DNA testing? Okay, two weeks then. I know. Two weeks is a long time, but it can't be helped." He paused a second before continuing. "Yes, I spoke with the Chief, and he was only a little ticked off that I didn't go through him before I asked you to test the tissue we found in Mom's car. He got over it though. Mom's charming voice rarely fails." Ralph smiled as he listened to the sound of Sam's voice. "Doing all right so far. How about you? Good." He listened again, then said, "Mom found the spot where it happened, so she's a little shaky right now. I know. Well, look, I got to run. Talk to you soon, Sam."

Twenty minutes later, two police cars and a vehicle from the lab arrived. Ralph placed his hand on his mother's shoulder. "I'll be back in a few minutes to take you home. Okay?"

"Don't worry about me, Ralph. I'll be fine."

Ralph met the team of people waiting for him. Twice, he sent someone to check on his mother. When they reported she was still sleeping, he continued to work with the team searching for evidence. On the third trip to his car, the officer informed him she was awake and looking rather pale. "Okay, thanks. I need to take her home."

Karl Ferrell stood nearby and spoke up. "Do you want me to take her home so you can stay, Ralph?"

"Thanks, Karl. But I need to do it in case she, well, in case she gets upset or something."

"Sure," Karl said. "She'll want you there."

Ralph trotted to the car and slid onto the driver's seat. One look told him the last officer to check on her was correct. She was pale and drawn. He turned the car around, then held his mother's hand as they drove to her house.

She lived near the edge of town in the house she bought eleven years ago for herself and the three boys. It was a two-story affair, but after the boys left, she converted a downstairs room into her bedroom so the upstairs was only used when one of the boys stayed with her. The acre of land was really too much for her, but Ralph and Teddy swapped weeks cutting the grass and maintaining the property.

When Ralph pulled into the driveway, Miss Treadwell relaxed for the first time in a week. She'd convinced them there actually was a murder. Now they were investigating. Her job was over. Her eyes took in the peace that surrounded the house and garden. "The roses," she said softly.

"Roses?"

"Yes, they need deadheading. I'll take care of that tomorrow. Did it rain while I was in the hospital?"

Ralph thought a moment. "No. It didn't rain."

"Then I need to water the flowers," Miss Treadwell said as she continued to survey all that she had planted and babied over the years. "Is the watering hose still hooked up, Ralph?"

The lines on Ralph's face softened as he realized her mind was returning to the living rather than lingering on the horror of what she'd just relived. What she experienced would never really leave her, but the fact she had shifted to the present was a start. "It's hooked up. Now, look, Mom. Teddy and I can do all that. You don't have to worry about cutting off the dead blooms on your rose bushes or watering your plants. I'll work it out with Teddy and one of us will take care of it."

Miss Treadwell patted his arm. "I know, dear. I'm just being a fusspot."

Ralph smiled as he got out of the car and came around to help his mother. "You are not a fusspot. You love your flowers, and you don't want them to die." He walked her to the front door, unlocked it, and turned to her with deep concern etched on his face. "Mom, I want you to keep all your doors and windows locked. Okay?"

"I understand. I promise to keep the house locked up tight."

"Good. Can I do anything for you before I leave? Are you hungry? I can make a sandwich for you."

"I'm not hungry right now. I'll make something a little later. Right now, I just need a hug."

Ralph's eyes stung as he embraced the woman who had spared him from a life of loneliness and destitution. "Lock your doors and windows," he said again. "I'm going to work something out so you won't be alone." When he sensed a protest about to erupt, he put up his hand.

"Sorry, Mom. It has to be this way."

At the end of the driveway, Ralph debated returning to the scene to see how it was progressing. They knew their job. They didn't need his help just yet. He turned in the opposite direction and headed into town. The most important thing right now was protecting Mom. She was the only mother he'd known. She was also their key witness. Their only witness. Keeping a witness safe and alive sometimes meant staying one step ahead of the people who wanted them dead. But would they be able to do that?

Mike inspected the dove he was carving out of wood. It was a delicate business keeping everything in perspective. Details. If his pocketknife slipped a tiny millimeter, the carving was tossed into the fire.

He looked up suddenly as he heard the door open. "Goin' some-where, Mister?"

"Into town."

"Why?"

"Do you mind? I don't need to report my movements to you."

Mike slowly sharpened his pocketknife. "Jist askin'. That's all. Gittin' another one of them there notebooks?"

"Among other things. There's business that needs taking care of."

"What kinda business?" Mike asked, testing the pocketknife for sharpness.

"I intend to buy a gift. Not that I owe you an explanation."

"Okay," Mike said. "I'll jist sit real quiet like and work on my dove."

Silky Voice paused a moment to study the boy with two faces. One had the appearance of normalcy. The other kept him awake at night sharpening his knife. "I'll be back in an hour or two."

Silky Voice parked on a side street and walked several blocks out of his way before doubling back. He waited until the shop was empty, pulled his cap farther down on his forehead, and slipped through the door. He knew exactly what he wanted, so it was a matter of wandering up and down the aisles until he located it. After slipping on a clear plastic glove, he picked up two boxes, laid the boxes on the counter then removed the plastic glove while the cashier made her way to the checkout counter. After the cashier placed the boxes inside a bag, he nodded his thanks, and left. In the privacy of the car, he slipped his hands inside plastic gloves, tore off the cellophane wrapper, and drew the syringe from his pocket. Afterwards, he debated which route to take. Once that was settled, he drove the back streets until he reached the main artery leading to Bedford. This wouldn't solve his problem, but it would buy him a little more time. Hopefully a little more time was all he needed.

Chapter 15

Ralph chose the same counter seat he had only that morning and waited for Teddy to make an appearance. Was it only this morning he was here waiting for Teddy to brew tea and make toast for Mom? Seemed like a week ago. It was the slow time of day, so Teddy would have a few minutes to talk.

The door leading to the kitchen swung open and Teddy walked through. He stopped short as he saw Ralph waiting for him.

"Mom okay?"

"She's all right, but I need to talk to you. Got a minute?"

"Sure, what's up?" Teddy said, his brows drawing together. "Coffee?"

"Thanks. I could use a cup." Ralph waited till Teddy was seated next to him with his own coffee. "I don't know what was going on in Mom's mind this morning, but suddenly she remembered you're one of her boys."

With those words, a tension he was unaware of left Teddy's

shoulders. "How do you know? What did she say?"

Ralph inhaled deeply. Where to begin? "Okay, let me bring you up to date on what's happened, and I'll tell you."

"Okay, tell me what happened."

"I just got back from taking her for a drive along Muddy Creek. We found the spot she was talking about. There's been a murder."

Teddy carefully placed his coffee cup on the counter while he stared at Ralph. "You're not serious?"

"Dead serious," Ralph said, then closed his eyes. "Sorry. Yes. There really was a murder." He took another sip of coffee while Teddy studied the lines of fatigue etched on his face.

"You need to rest, bud."

"Can't. At least not yet," Ralph said. "After I left here, Mom drank her tea and asked me if we'd checked her car. When I said we hadn't, she took me around the corner where her car was parked and there was a tissue tucked along the bottom of the driver's seat. Sam analyzed it and found traces of ether. That was the first thing that happened."

Teddy's mouth went dry. "Ether?" he whispered. "Someone wanted to keep her quiet for a while. But ether wouldn't keep her asleep very long, would it?"

"No. She remembers someone rolling up her left sleeve and a sharp jab like a needle."

"Someone injected Mom with something to knock her out?! And to think we didn't believe her." Teddy rested his head in his hands as he visualized how the event must have unfolded. Finally, he turned to gaze at Ralph. No wonder the man looked tired. "What else?"

"Do you remember when I told you the photos were not on her camera's memory card?"

"Sure, I remember. That's the main reason you felt her memory of the murder was the result of the concussion and didn't really happen."

"Yeah, well get this. Sam said the memory card in her camera has only been available for sale in the past six months. Mom bought her memory card about two years ago."

"It wasn't Mom's memory card."

"Somebody replaced her memory card with a new one and reshot photos while she was asleep," Ralph said. "When we were at the lab talking to Sam, she mentioned you were one of her boys and that your birthday was the month after mine. She even mentioned Bobby. So, I don't know why she seemed unable to make the connection when we were in the Chief's office. She wanted me to get tea and toast for her across the street. That's when she said, 'You remember Teddy Clearfield, don't you?' She seems back to normal for the most part. Exhausted as you can imagine."

They sipped their coffee, immersed in their own thoughts. Finally, Teddy said, "What are we going to do?"

"Well, first of all, we have to cut the grass, deadhead her roses, and water her plants."

The men smiled while they shook their heads. "Nothing defeats this woman!" Teddy said.

"Nothing!" Ralph said, "Look, Teddy. You realize Mom may be in danger, right?

"Of course!" Teddy said, sobering up immediately. "I'll move in there tonight."

"Maybe we can switch nights. But what about days?"

Teddy gave Ralph a sly look. "Could Sam switch to another shift and spend days with her?"

"Hm," Ralph said, trying, unsuccessfully, to hide a smile. "She might."

"Want me to call and ask?"

"No. I'll call her. I'll call her on my way back to the murder scene." He finished his coffee and patted Teddy's shoulder on his way to the door. After Ralph slipped behind the wheel of his car, he sat for a moment. Should he check in with the Chief? Better wait until he had something more to report than they were searching the scene for evidence. Instead, he called the lab. "Sam?"

"Are you all right?" Sam said, detecting the strain in his voice. "Has something happened?"

"I'm all right," Ralph said. "Just talked to Teddy, and we're a little worried about Mom."

"I'd be worried, too," Sam said. "Actually, I am worried."

"Worried about Mom? Is that what you mean?"

"I don't know why I'm holding back. You already know this. Your mother is the only witness. She's in danger. She's been in danger from the moment she found the body. We just didn't realize it."

"I know. Teddy and I are both worried about it. We're going to trade nights staying there."

"But you don't have anyone for the daytime."

"Well, not yet."

"Look, Ralph. It's easy for me to change shifts. I could be with your mother while you and Teddy work."

"You'd be willing to do that?" Ralph said, relief flooding his voice.

"Of course I would," Sam said, a smile in her voice despite everything. "I'll start tomorrow. Okay?"

"Thanks, Sam. That means a lot."

"I know."

It was later in the afternoon when a customer walked into the café. A few people were scattered around the café drinking coffee, occupied on their phones, or focused on the person seated across the table from them.

He wore a baseball cap pulled down low over his forehead. A pair of sunglasses was perched on his nose. Instead of a table or booth, he chose a stool at the very end of the counter near the front door. He hunched over, staring unseeing at the newspaper he'd brought with him.

Teddy walked around the counter and smiled. "What can I get you?"

"Just black coffee."

Teddy made fresh coffee, casting glances at his customer, wondering who he was. "Here you are," Teddy said. "Anything to eat?"

"No, thanks," the man said softly.

"New in town?"

"Sort of," the man said. "Lived here when I was a kid. Haven't been back since."

"Oh, that's interesting," Teddy said, since there wasn't much else to say about it.

"Yes, lived just out of town. It was a quiet place to live. Nothing exciting ever happened. Pretty much the same thing every day.

Has it changed much in the last fifteen years? Is it still fairly quiet and peaceful?"

"Was until recently," Teddy said, shaking his head.

"Oh, what do you mean?"

"Person got murdered."

"Murdered? What happened?"

"Not sure," Teddy said. "My brother is on the police force, and they've just had new evidence, so they've reopened the case. It'll be in the newspapers tomorrow. You can count on it."

"Your brother is a policeman. You probably know all about it then."

Teddy smiled evasively. "No, Ralph is pretty tight-lipped about stuff like that. I only know what I hear on the news or read in the paper."

"No leads? Don't they have any idea what happened or who murdered the poor guy?"

"Not yet. They're working on it. Something will come up. Usually does," Teddy said. "Interesting you haven't heard anything about it."

The man shrugged his shoulders. "Been away on vacation. Mostly fishing and staying in a cabin in the woods. Haven't listened to the news or read anything."

"Oh, well that explains it."

"Shame about the murder. Hope you find the guys who were responsible for it," the man said. He paid his bill and stood ready to leave.

"I hope they do, too. Stop in again," Teddy called out as the man opened the door. He cleared away the coffee cup and prepared for the dinner crowd. By ten o'clock, he dealt with things that could only be done when there were no customers to interrupt him.

Teddy lived above the café. After he locked the front door for the night, he dragged his feet up the stairs to his apartment. It was after he finished his hot shower and climbed into bed that the realization hit him. He hadn't mentioned whether the murdered person was a man or woman, yet the stranger referred to the body as "the guy" and "the man being murdered". And how did he know there was more than one suspect? Because he'd said, "Hope you find the guys who were responsible for it." Finally, he decided there was nothing in it and he was looking for a reason to be suspicious when none existed.

Chapter 16

October 4, 1995

It was Teddy's third morning sleeping in his old bed and sitting across the breakfast table from his mom. The paleness was gone, and her level of energy had returned. When his cell phone buzzed, he replaced his teacup in its saucer and answered. Immediately, he shot out of his chair. "Have you got it contained yet?" He sighed. "Okay, I'll be there in ten minutes."

"What is it, Teddy?" his mother said, following him to her front door.

"Sorry, Mom. That was the fire department. A fire started in the kitchen at the café. No idea how that could have happened, but I've got to run down there and see what's going on." Teddy glanced at his watch as he headed for his car. "Sam won't be here for an hour. Why don't you come with me? I think that's what Ralph would want us to do."

"Oh, Teddy. I'm no good with fires. I'd just be in the way. Besides, I haven't finished my tea yet. You run along. I'll be fine until Sam gets here."

Teddy gave his mother a quick kiss. "Keep your doors locked. I'll check in with you as soon as I can. Okay?"

"Now, Teddy, I can look after myself, so don't worry about me," she said firmly but with a smile. "In any case, I brought my garden shovel in from the potting shed. Ralph sharpened it for me a few weeks ago, so I'm prepared for any eventuality."

In spite of the fire, Teddy kissed her again, backed out of the driveway, and sped away.

The washing up had just been completed when the doorbell rang. It was still too early for Sam. Not that she needed all this babysitting. Even so, she grabbed her shovel and headed cautiously for the door. She looked through the side window and saw a post office delivery van. She rested her shovel in the corner beside the door within easy reach. "Hello," she said as she cracked open the chained door.

"Delivery, ma'am. Need you to sign for it."

Miss Treadwell studied the man as he offered the clipboard for her signature. He wore his delivery cap low on his head which didn't help. The fact that his chin was tilted down didn't help either. "I wonder who sent this?"

"Bobby something shipped it from California. Last name isn't clear."

"Bobby! One of my boys. How nice. I can't imagine what he's sending me this time of year. Ralph or Teddy must have called him and now he's worried about me." She relaxed, opened the door, and signed for the box. With one last futile attempt to see what he looked like, she said, "Thank you very much."

"Yes, ma'am," the man said. He walked rapidly to the van, pulled out of the driveway, and headed in the direction leading out of town.

She gave the door a careless shove and sat down in her favorite chair. As she cut through the paper, something nagged at her. That voice. It was the smooth, silky voice she remembered. The one who said, "Murder? What murder? Body you say. Have you called the police yet?" He asked if the camera on the floor was the one she used. He must have been the one who rolled up her sleeve and injected her arm, because Mike was quite busy wiping the nonexistent blood off her face.

Feeling a bit shaky, she leaned back heavily on her chair. They'd found her. Ralph and Teddy's worst fears had been realized. All the precautions were for nothing. Now they knew where she lived, and it was just a matter of time before.... But why hadn't the man just done away with her that very instant? It would have been so simple, so much cleaner. Why drop off this silly box and leave?

Another crushing thought pressed to the forefront. How did he know about Bobby, her third son from the group home for boys? She swallowed hard. Bobby lived in California. So far away, yet he mentioned his name and the state where he lived.

Her hands shook as these thoughts raced through her mind. She recalled the sting of the injection. Worse by far was the missing memory card from her camera. Those shots of the murdered man. Gone forever, she fumed and shook her head.

Suddenly, she realized he was getting away. She was allowing their only chance of capturing the murderer to escape. They knew where she lived. She had nothing to lose. Leaving the box in the shadow of the chair, she grabbed her purse from the hallway closet as well as her camera resting beside it. Her phone. She grabbed it off the hall table and dropped it into her purse. By sheer instinct, she threw a jacket over her shoulder and walked rapidly into the kitchen where she lifted her car key off a hook. Through the door and down the steps she trotted to the garage.

This was not the time to worry about seatbelts. She turned on the ignition, but only silence followed, so she tried again. That was another silence-filled moment. For exactly one second, she recalled the conversation with Ralph, who offered to make the appointment with the garage. Too late to worry about spilt milk now.

With renewed determination, she gave her engine one more try. This time, it turned over. She backed her car, rather mindlessly, out of the garage, creating a matching dent to its twin on the other side. Squealing out of the driveway, she headed in the direction of the van. Challenging the speed limit had never greatly concerned her in the past, and it didn't concern her now. Within forty seconds, she had the van in sight.

Miss Treadwell had read enough mystery books to know that on no account should she tail the suspect too closely. In fact, keeping one or two cars between her and the van was an absolute must. She had no trouble keeping her distance or cars between them until they were well into the countryside and traffic sped up and thinned out. Her foot let up on the accelerator and the car drifted back, allowing more space between her and the person who was surely a murderer.

Even with increasing the distance, he may have spotted her. Dropping back farther still, she added another two hundred feet to the gap. There was a narrowing of her brows as they reached the edge of the wooded area. Through breaks in the trees, she saw the glint of sun off water. Her pulse increased as she recognized where they were heading.

With every twist in the road, Miss Treadwell lost sight of the delivery van. She fought the temptation to increase her speed and was rewarded when she reached a straightaway and spotted him in the distance.

When the next curve in the road straightened, she had gained on him considerably. Why had he slowed down? There were no roads he could pull onto along this stretch. She let up on the accelerator and pressed gently on her brakes.

The van came to a full stop and remained there. What was he doing? Quickly, she pulled as far onto the wide berm as possible without her wheels sliding into the ditch. She was far enough to the right that she couldn't see his side mirror, which meant he couldn't see her either.

Suddenly, the driver made a quick ninety-degree turn, pulled off the road and disappeared. Was there a narrow path she knew nothing about?

Was this near the scene of her accident? She couldn't be sure, yet it looked so familiar from the day she and Ralph drove past it. There was a cutout large enough to be a rest stop right about there. Did some type of path lead away from where her car collided with the tree? She didn't remember. Her memory of that day came back in small chunks and at the oddest times. Until a short time ago, no one believed a murder actually occurred. She knew the investigators were still at the scene of the murder along Muddy Creek. But had they checked the scene of her car crash? She had no idea. Why hadn't she asked Ralph about it?

Should she sit tight and wait in case he reappeared and continued on? Had he spotted her? Was that why he pulled over?

Did she dare inch forward to check for a dirt path? Or had the driver seen her and pulled over to draw her into a trap? Miss Treadwell tapped the steering wheel with her fingertips. The smartest thing to do was call Ralph. She reached inside her purse for her phone, opened her purse wider, and rummaged through it. Finally, she dumped out its entire contents onto the seat. She dropped her head onto her chest. In her haste, she thought she placed the phone inside her purse. She hadn't heard it hit the floor, but it was carpeted and her mind was on tailing the suspect. Now it was too late. She could return to Bedford, but the driver may very well pull out and keep going. On the other hand, if she pressed forward, he may be waiting for her.

Drawing a deep, sustaining breath, she searched the area ahead and behind her. In her rearview mirror, she spotted a wider berm. If she backed up carefully, she could pull safely off the road. Once there, she turned off the car and continued to plan.

She'd make her way beside the road, but if this was a trap, she'd walk right into it. The woods. It was better to make her way through the woods at an angle, hoping to spot the van through the trees before Silky Voice saw her. Then she could drive to the nearest gas station, give Ralph a quick call, and report what she'd found.

After returning everything to her purse that was currently scattered about the car seat, she picked up her camera from its cushion on the floor. Drawing the straps of her camera and purse over her shoulder, Miss Treadwell eased out of the car. Jacket. It might just get chilly before this day was over. She slipped on her jacket, quietly closed the door, and disappeared into the cover of the trees.

Chapter 17

As Sam turned into Miss Treadwell's street, she saw Teddy squealing around the corner from the opposite direction. He sprinted for the house, tripped halfway, regained his balance, and burst through the unlocked door.

Something unexpected and alarming had happened. After parking behind Teddy's car, Sam bolted through the open front door.

Teddy wheeled around and closed his eyes.

"Teddy! What is it? Has something happened to your mother?"

"She's gone!" Teddy said, his voice a reflection of his state of mind.

"Gone? Do you think she's been kidnapped? Should we call Ralph?"

Teddy opened his hand. Resting in his palm was his mother's phone. "It was on the floor when I walked in."

"Her phone?"

Teddy nodded. "There's more."

Sam saw a mixture of guilt, worry, and shock written on his face. She took his arm and led him to the couch and sat down beside him. "Tell me what happened."

Teddy swallowed as he stared at the floor. "I got a phone call. The man said the kitchen at the café had caught fire. I needed to get there immediately," he said, then turned to meet Sam's eyes. "So I left. I knew you'd be here shortly and told Mom to keep the doors locked."

"There was no fire."

"No fire."

"The front door didn't appear to be locked."

"No, it wasn't. It was slightly ajar. She must have opened the door and failed to close it completely. Or someone grabbed her and didn't shut the door," Teddy said. "She's been so careful about locking it. What could have happened that she forgot?"

"Have you checked through the house?"

Teddy looked up with a trace of hope in his eyes. "No. When I saw her phone on the floor, I assumed the worst. I'll take the upstairs; you cover the main floor. Okay?"

"Right."

Teddy returned to see his worried look reflected in Sam's eyes. "Basement!" he said with the tiniest shred of hope. He crashed down the stairs, but his plodding return needed no explanation.

Sam didn't need to ask. "Where does she keep her purse?"

"In the hall closet." It took ten seconds to realize her purse was gone. "She took her camera, too."

"Does she usually take her camera wherever she goes?" Sam said.

"Always. Even if she's only going to the grocery store," Teddy said.

"If someone kidnapped her, she wouldn't have taken her purse or her camera. So, she drove somewhere of her own free will."

"Would she leave without locking the front door?"

"Never, unless something extraordinary happened."

"Something extraordinary did happen so she broke from her usual routine," Sam said. "But did she take her own car when she left?"

"I'm not thinking. I should have checked the garage when I first got here." Teddy rounded the corner where his mother kept her car keys on a hook beside the back door. "Keys are gone. Let's check the garage."

Teddy and Sam stood side by side at the entrance to the garage, staring at the oil drip where the car usually stood.

As they hurried back to the house, Teddy fought to keep his emotions in check so his mind could logically think through possibilities and how to proceed. Yet how could he call Ralph and tell him he'd been an utter fool and fallen for such an obvious ruse?

"I can't just stand here doing nothing!" Teddy tapped his fist on the countertop in the kitchen. "I want to leave and start searching, but we have no idea where to go!"

Sam studied him for a moment. "Coffee or tea?"

Teddy raised an eyebrow then slowly smiled. "Tea. Thanks." He sat down heavily on a kitchen chair and reached for his phone. "Ralph? Mom's disappeared. Someone called. Said the café kitchen was on fire. I was caught off guard, but that's no excuse for leaving her." He listened for a moment "I know. Oldest trick in the book and I fell for it. She took her car but forgot her phone. Well, she didn't forget it. It was in the middle of the floor. Must have slid out of her hand or pocket. That's the problem. What do you want us to do?" Teddy listened while Ralph responded. "Right, Sam's here. There's got to be something I can do." He dropped his head and murmured, "Okay."

"What did Ralph say?"

"He said to sit tight in case she comes home."

"That's not going to be easy to do."

"No."

"Did Ralph say what he was going to do?" Sam said.

"No, and I didn't want to ask. He'll do whatever he can. Probably put out an all-points bulletin or whatever they call it."

"Did he sound upset?"

Teddy sighed. "Yes. Ralph's not upset with me. He said he would have done the same thing. I own a café. What do I know about stuff like this?"

Sam placed tea on the table and sat across from Teddy. "The hardest part is to wait. I'll stay with you."

Teddy studied Sam and decided Ralph had chosen well. "Thanks."

They sipped their tea in silence, then gathered the dishes and placed them beside the sink. Feeling utterly useless, they wandered into the living room and sat down on opposite chairs. Teddy propped his head on his fist, while Sam considered how to best deal with the situation.

Sam studied photos of the boys' growing-up years. Her eyes drifted to another group of photos highlighting their high school graduation. Out of the corner of her eye, she saw a box hidden in the shadow of a chair. "What's this?"

Teddy followed the direction of her gaze and they rose together. He picked up the box and opened it, while Sam inspected the wrapping. "Chocolate candy," he said. "Mom loves the stuff, but it's not her birthday or Mother's Day or anything. Why would someone send it?"

"Looks like it's from Bobby," Sam said. "I can't read the last name."

"Bobby? I didn't call him when Mom was in the hospital because I didn't want to worry him. Ralph must have called to let him know. I wonder why he didn't tell me he called Bobby?"

"She mentioned Bobby briefly while she and Ralph were at the lab."

"Bobby grew up with us at the group home then all four of us moved into this house together. He moved to the west coast soon after he left college. I've never known him to send Mom gifts except on special occasions. He must have heard she was in the hospital and sent this to her. Maybe I should call Ralph and ask him if he spoke with Bobby." Teddy studied the floor for a moment while he thought. "He's too busy to hear about Bobby and why he sent candy."

Sam inspected the wrapping, "There's no return address. Miss Treadwell's name and address are clearly written, and Bobby's first name is clearly written. Why did he scribble his last name so it's impossible to read?"

"Let me see." Teddy paled significantly as he studied the wrapping. "This isn't Bobby's handwriting."

Chapter 18

Teddy continued to stare at the writing on the wrapping paper. "It came through the post office. Our mailbox is large. This package would fit inside it," he said, his face a study in confusion.

"What is it, Teddy?"

Teddy looked up. "It's too early for the mail to be delivered. And if she saw the mail carrier deliver the mail, she would have brought in the rest of the mail with this box." He made a quick check of the downstairs and the wastebasket. "No mail has been tossed out. Let me check if it arrived earlier today. Maybe she just didn't bring in the rest of it. Doesn't make sense, but you never know." Within a moment, he returned to the house, shaking his head. "No mail yet."

"No mail," Sam murmured. She stepped to the window to gain a better perspective of the outside wrapping paper.

"What is it? What are you looking for?"

"This looks very much like it came through the regular post office, but the markings are off just enough that I'm not sure it has actually gone through the post office. The cancellation mark is good, but not perfect."

"You mean somebody did this deliberately to avoid arousing suspicion? But who could have sent this? And why?" He reached for a piece of the candy.

"Wait!" Sam said.

"What's wrong? I just wanted to get a closer look at it."

"I know. I'm sorry. I wasn't trying to startle you. Since we don't know who sent this or why, we need to find out if the candy has been tampered with. And the sooner the better."

"Tampered with? You mean like poison or something like that?"

"I'm not saying poisoned, just tampered with."

"Okay. I get it. What should we do?"

"Does your mother have a magnifying glass?" Sam said.

"She keeps it inside a drawer beside her chair." He produced the magnifying glass and waited for Sam's next move.

"I need plastic gloves to handle the candy. There's probably some for the washing up."

"Actually, Ralph keeps gloves for bagging evidence in the kitchen. That's even better, right?"

"Yes, evidence gloves are a lot better. Ralph's gloves will be a little large for my hands, but they're better suited for picking up evidence."

"Evidence?" Teddy said. "Of course. I understand." He led the way to the kitchen where evidence gloves were produced from a side drawer.

They stood side by side while Sam donned the gloves and carefully lifted a piece of chocolate from the box. She held it under the magnifying glass slowly turning it until every millimeter had been inspected. She did that with every piece of candy until she reached the eleventh piece. "Look, Teddy. Do you see this spot right here?"

Teddy leaned over the magnifying glass, then straightened up. His face was drawn as he turned to Sam. "There's a tiny hole in it."

Sam waited while Teddy internalized the significance of the hole.

"Somebody injected poison into the candy? Is that what you think?"

"Possibly." Sam never speculated. "I need to look at the rest of the candy." After examining the rest of the candy, she replaced the lid.

"The rest of the candy is all right then?" Teddy said. "The eleventh piece is the only one poisoned?"

"I don't know if the candy has been poisoned. I won't know until I test it. At least, the first ten pieces appear undisturbed as well as the rest of the candy following that," Sam said. "But just because the others haven't been visually disturbed, doesn't mean they haven't been tampered with."

"Okay. Say all the candy is fine except the eleventh one. Why poison only one piece?"

"Did you notice the eleventh piece of candy is somewhere close to the middle of the box?"

"Yes, I noticed it was near the middle. Is that important?"

Sam pulled her thoughts together before proceeding. "Suppose the goal was to poison the only witness who can identify the possible suspects to the murder. You with me?"

"I'm with you."

"Okay. Now, your mother is seventy. She's healthy and gets around like someone much younger than herself. But people her age can die suddenly for a number of reasons which can be attributed to deadly attacks which have nothing to do with outside intervention. You still with me?"

"Still with you," Teddy said, but his mind refused to accept the theory that Sam was presenting to him.

"If you poison all the candy, it would be an obvious case of murder. But if you poison only one piece, when the rest of the candy is analyzed without positive results for poison, then it strengthens the case that sudden death could be attributed to a heart attack or a massive stroke."

Teddy sat down on the nearest chair. "What kind of people are we dealing with?" he said softly. "It's so utterly diabolic and cruel."

Sam sat on the opposite chair. "I know. I've seen so much of it, but this is your first encounter with horrific crimes and I'm sure it's a shock for you. And she's your mother."

Teddy nodded. "Reading about it and having it happen to someone you love are two different things."

"Of course, it's very different." Sam allowed Teddy a few moments to internalize what was happening. "Teddy?" When he looked up, she continued, "I need to put everything inside a bag or box and take it to the lab right away. And, uh, you need to call Ralph and tell him what we found. Okay?"

"Right, I understand," Teddy said. He grabbed a plastic bag from inside a drawer and a box from the basement. "Will these do?"

"Perfect," Sam said. They bagged the box of candy and wrapping paper and headed quickly to her car.

"How long will it take you to find out what's in the candy?"

"Not long, I hope."

"Will you call me as soon as you find out?"

Sam's eyes revealed sympathy for this man whose mother was missing and whose life may very well be in danger. "Don't worry, Teddy. I'll call Ralph first, then I'll call you right after that. Okay?"

"Okay, thanks." Teddy stood watching as Sam backed out of the driveway and sped away into town.

Mike looked up as the door opened. "Been gone a long time, Mister," he said. "Where ya been?"

"In town."

"Better not show yer face around these here little towns, 'cause ever'body knows ever'body. They'll spot ya as not belongin' there."

"You think I'm stupid?"

"Not stupid. Maybe a touch o' crazy," Mike said. He picked up his pocketknife, checked for imperfections in his work, then continued carving the figure of a dove. "What was ya doin'?"

"Shopping."

"Shoppin'?" Mike said, glancing warily at the other man. "Find anythin'?"

"Hopefully."

"What's that s'posed ta mean?"

"It means I hope my plan works. In any case, I decided to buy two of them rather than just one."

Mike waited, continuing to stare while assessing the other man's mood and motive. "Gonna tell me what ya bought?"

"Sure," Silky Voice said. "I bought something for you."

Ever cautious, Mike said, "Fer me? What is it?"

Silky Voice reached into a bag and handed it to Mike. "A box of chocolate candy."

Mike opened the box and ate the first piece.

Chapter 19

Ten minutes of stepping over fallen branches and treading on uneven ground left Miss Treadwell feeling a bit weary. What became increasingly tiring was avoiding anything that made a crunching or snapping sound. Why had she thought this was such a good idea? Even if she came face to face with Mike and Silky Voice, just what could she possibly do about it? Make a citizen's arrest? Hardly! Well, snapping a photo of them would be partial justice for that poor murdered man.

She dropped down on an absolutely filthy tree stump, but she was in no position to be fussy about it. Ten minutes of rest. That's how much time she allotted herself. Amazingly, that ten minutes did her a world of good and she pressed on.

She stopped and tilted her head. A new sound drifted through the trees. Was it animal or human? Directions were so unreliable in the woods. Cautiously, she moved forward, even more watchful of any step that may reveal her presence. There it was again. Except this time she recognized a human voice. No. Two voices. Not much farther, if only she could draw nearer without being detected.

They were arguing. Arguing voices are more difficult to recognize. Everything changes with an angry voice. Although, if they were angry, they would be so involved and focused on each other, they may not hear someone approaching. Even so, she calculated each step with great care.

Now there was but a short distance between her and the open ground. She slipped behind a line of scrubby shrubs and slowly parted them. Twenty feet away, she spotted the van that had parked in her driveway nearly an hour ago.

The two men were some distance from the van but not so far away she couldn't hear their raised voices. Even through the haze of her accident over two weeks ago, she recognized one of them. His hair stuck out in every conceivable direction and his skin still maintained that pasty look. Mike. Now, she saw how very young he was. Possibly still a teenager. When the other man spoke, she recognized his voice as well, since she'd heard it reflected in the delivery man.

Miss Treadwell listened, her brows slowly drawing together.

"Look. This is the last time I'm asking you nicely. Where did you hide them?"

Mike raised the ax and brought it down, splitting the block of wood in two. "Why ya wanna know?"

Silky Voice scoffed. "Don't you think I have a right to know?"

"Maybe. Maybe not. Have ta think 'bout it."

Silky Voice paced back and forth in front of the pile of wood Mike was splitting. "I need to know in the event something, well, something happens to you."

Mike lowered his ax. "You plan on somethin' happenin' ta me?"

"No, of course not! Don't be ridiculous! I need you. You know that."

"I know ya need me right now. But if I tell ya where they is, you might not need me so much. And that's why I'm not tellin' ya. Besides. It's ugly."

Silky Voice resumed pacing. Once again, he stopped in front of the pile of wood. "We're partners, right? That's what we decided, right?"

"That's what you decided. I don't want no parts of it."

He rested his hands on his hips. "And just what do you mean by that?"

"Well, Mister," Mike began, gauging how much force he needed to split the next block of wood. "I jist wanna go 'bout my business and not havta worry 'bout nothin'."

"What if I offer you more money? What would you think then?"

Mike stared at the other man a few seconds, then used his thumb to test the sharpness of the ax. "I dunno. I don't like bein' bought."

"Okay. What if I offer you a lot of money? Enough that you won't have to worry about money for a very long time."

Never have ta worry about money for a very long time, Mike thought as he lifted the ax over his head. "I dunno. I gotta think 'bout it."

"Yes, well, you think about it. All you have to do is tell me the whereabouts of the car and the body."

Miss Treadwell couldn't make out precisely what they were saying because they were quite a distance away, but it unnerved her greatly that she clearly heard the last two words, "the body". She began to wonder if she was truly capable of seeing this through. Perhaps she should slip away and allow the professionals, the people who actually knew what they were doing, take over. But she couldn't return empty-handed. As before, she'd take a few photos and leave.

She looked beyond the men to a small cabin. Was this their hideout? Most likely. A tiny wince of pain escaped her lips when her knee came in contact with a sharp-edged twig. What was that? She heard a similar sound coming from the van just a few feet away. The men's voices were raised to the point where they hadn't heard it.

She couldn't permit little mysteries to distract her. Miss Treadwell laid her purse carefully aside, removed the lens cover, and slipped it into her pocket. Raising the camera to her eye, she rotated the lens, and pressed halfway down on the shutter button. When their faces came into focus, she captured several shots in a row. Moving the camera slightly to the right, she took several photos of the cabin, and the van.

There was that sound again. The sound was a duplicate of the shutter button taking photos. Did she dare test it? The men took a break from arguing. Once they resumed, she took a handful of leaves and crunched them. She froze when the echo of crunched leaves came from the van.

The seemingly impossible can come as a slower revelation than the obvious. They had planted a tiny microphone on her purse which was received somewhere inside that van. That's how Mike and Silky Voice knew her every move.

Miss Treadwell drew her hand to her chest as she realized that's how they knew about Bobby. Bobby's name had been mentioned in the lab when she spoke with Sam. They used Bobby's name on the package containing candy because he was the only one of her boys who lived far enough away to mail something to her. The boys. Those men knew all about her boys. But she mustn't think about that right now or permit that knowledge to defeat her, or all would be lost. She closed her eyes. What to do? What to do?

The one thing she absolutely could not do was be captured. She waited until their voices were particularly loud, then replaced the lens cover and drew the strap of her purse over her shoulder. Slowly, she rose and retraced her steps. She hadn't gone fifty feet when Mike said, "What was that? Did you hear it?"

Chapter 20

Miss Treadwell struggled to put distance between herself and the two men. She heard the van door open and close. Even in her panic, she wondered why they'd stopped to do that. A gun? That thought gave her the adrenaline rush she needed to press on.

Behind her came the sound of crunching leaves and twigs. They had narrowed the distance.

Think! If she couldn't outrun them, then she must outsmart them. What would they expect her to do? Where would they expect her to go? The road. Of course! They'd expect her to make a run for the car and escape.

Shifting her direction, she headed deeper into the woods. It became increasingly darker and denser. She was almost grateful. It forced her to slow down. Her breath came in short spurts. No one was directly behind her, but breathing so loudly, she really couldn't be sure. She stopped and held her breath as long as possible. All she heard was the chirping of birds and the playful squeals of squirrels fussing with each other.

She came upon the perfect hiding place. It was a sharp dip in the ground that cut back into the earth, creating a space just large enough for her body. She slid down the embankment and covered up the parallel lines on the ground revealing where she'd gone. She drew leaves and twigs in with her as she crawled into the small area. When all was arranged as tightly as possible, Miss Treadwell could see nothing beyond the enclosed cave she'd created for herself. But then, she thought hopefully, they couldn't see her either.

Leaning back, she closed her eyes and sighed. But her eyes snapped opened as she heard that sigh echoing nearby. It was the same echo she heard when she shot the photos. The microphone. They'd found her.

Teddy dropped his head, walked back into the house, and sat heavily on a kitchen chair staring at his phone. Ralph. Calling him would add immeasurably to the burden he already carried. Slowly, Teddy picked up his phone and waited for his brother to answer.

"Look, I know you're busy, but something's come up, and you need to know about it." He waited until his voice was under control before giving a detailed report of the morning. Teddy heard the exhausted despair in his brother's response. It was just one more critical detail in the investigation. And it was personal. "There's no reason for you to remember this, but did you think of the evidence gloves I keep in the kitchen?"

"Yes, Sam asked for gloves, and I remembered you always kept some in a kitchen drawer. I got a box from the basement. She put the candy and wrappings in it and took it to the lab. She'll call you as soon as she's tested it."

Ralph had stepped away from the team of people working at the scene of the investigation. He considered the possibilities. "I think you should pack up and leave the house. Leave immediately. I don't like you being there by yourself. I know, but I can call you from wherever I am. As soon as we're done talking, get out. Okay? Leave a note just in case, I mean when Mom returns, and the house is empty." He listened then dropped his head. "I don't know. I don't have any idea where she is or where to start looking. The entire state has a description of Mom and her car, so we should know soon, I hope. Anyway, pack up and leave right now. Okay? Good. I'll get back to you when I find something."

Ralph stood where he was, his eyes focused yet unseeing on the staff at work. His focus narrowed as Jody rose to her feet holding a small object in a gloved hand. It was the look on the officer's face that increased his pace. When he reached her side, he said, "What have you got, Jody?"

"The pen Miss Treadwell mentioned. We've already taken photos. There's writing on the side."

Ralph slipped on a pair of gloves and carefully took possession of the pen. He drew it closer to his eyes, squinting in the daylight. "Cameron County District Attorney's Office," he said. "Where did you find it?"

Jody led him to a spot just behind the front tire marks where the driver's side door would have opened. "Right here. It was buried fairly deep as if someone stepped on it and ground it into the dirt."

"I wonder if he meant for us to find it, or was it just an accident?"

"I thought that, too. Deliberate or accident?"

"Let's take it to the lab. When they're finished with it, ask them to send it for DNA testing. Thanks, Jody. Good work. I'm going to call the district attorney's office right now and see what I can find out."

Ralph sat in his car and searched for the number of the Cameron County District Attorney's Office. He pressed the call number and waded through all the choices he had to make to reach someone who would actually answer the phone. "Hello? This is Detective Lieutenant Ralph Davies of the Bedford Police Department. I need to talk to someone in personnel, please." Once he was connected to the personnel office and identified himself, he said, "Look, we're investigating a probable murder, but there's no body so we can't confirm who it is or if there actually was a murder. We're at the scene and just found a pen. It was buried beside where a car was parked. It has Cameron County District Attorney's Office written on it."

"What?" the woman said. "You don't think someone from this office was murdered, do you?"

"That's the purpose of my call. This pen is the first piece of evidence we've found to connect the body with the actual person."

"I see." The woman sighed deeply. "By the way, my name is Carol. What do you want to know?"

"Is a white male between thirty and forty-five missing from your office or on vacation? Can you check on that for me while I wait?" he said, emphasizing the words "while I wait".

"White male between thirty and forty-five?" Carol said, her voice tight with tension. "I knew it. I knew it would end like this if he didn't pull back."

Chapter 21

Ralph gripped the phone as the shock of what Carol said settled upon him. "What do you mean by that? Who should have pulled back and why?" he said, then waited so long he worried she may have disconnected the call. "Are you still there?"

"I'm still here. Look, I was just muttering on about something. I didn't mean anything by it," Carol said, her voice a study in covering up her careless remark. "Anyway, I can't give out that kind information to the general public. How do I know you're from the Bedford Police Department?"

Ralph closed his eyes. "Would you feel more comfortable calling my boss? His name is Chief Henry Henderson. You can reach him at the Bedford Police Station right now if you want to verify who I am."

Carol hesitated. "Well, I guess I can give you a little general information."

"Good, I'd appreciate that."

"Give me a few minutes to check the men who fit that description, and I'll be back with you." Moments later, Carol reconnected. "Okay, I'm sorry to keep you waiting."

"That's all right. What did you find?"

"Three men who fit that description are on vacation right now. Everybody on staff is accounted for, which means nobody is actually missing."

When no further information was forthcoming, Ralph said, "And those three men fit the description, right?"

"Right. I just said they did."

"Of course. Just verifying. What can you tell me about them?"

The question was met with momentary silence. "I can't give you a lot of information, but I can tell you this. Of the three men on vacation, two of them are working on their houses right now, so I know they're not, uh, the possible victim."

"What about the third man?"

"Now, the third one I'm not too sure about. There's a bit of a mystery about John. I mean the third man. I can give you the District Attorney's Administrative Assistant if you like."

"That's perfect. Can you put me through to that person?"

"Yes, I can do that. Hold on. I think I mentioned my name is Carol in case you need to call back."

"Yes, you did. Thanks, Carol," Ralph said. He tapped his fingertips on the steering wheel as he gazed at the team continuing to examine the surrounding area. Two officers had actually stepped into the shallow water searching for clues. He glanced at his watch and thought of his mother. Where was she? Was she hurt or unconscious? Was she still alive? He should be doing something to find her, but the entire county was looking for her right now, so what could he add by leaving here?

"District Attorney's Office, Mark Jurvic," said a male voice.

"Hello, this is Detective Lieutenant Ralph Davies of the Bedford Police Department."

His speech was cut off suddenly when the assistant said, "Carol, the woman you spoke to in Personnel, told me who you are. She mentioned a pen with our office's name stamped on it and you have a probable murder with no body. Did I get that right?"

"That's right." Ralph scribbled the words "Mark Jurvic, AA to the Cameron County DA" below Carol's name.

"I can see this is a very difficult situation," Mark said in a strained voice. "Sorry to keep you waiting but I called Chief Henderson to verify. You understand?"

"Of course. I would do the same thing."

"How can I help you?" Mark said.

"I was told three men who match the description are on vacation. Two men are accounted for, but the third man is not. I'm wondering if there's any connection between the man who dropped this pen and the third man. Do you know where he is, or have you heard from him?"

"I just hope you're wrong about this," Mark said.

Wrong about this? "I understand. I hope I'm wrong, too. But I really need to pursue this line of inquiry and I need your help to do so."

"His name is John. John Calisto. He was working on a special case. Has to do with organized crime. He left here two weeks ago, and we haven't heard from him since."

"You haven't heard from Calisto in two weeks?" Ralph said, then checked his calendar. "So that would be about September nineteenth or twentieth?"

Mark Jurvic hesitated as he also checked his notes. "Yes. John called in, said he wanted to take vacation time starting immediately. We haven't heard from him since September twentieth."

September twentieth. And Mom found the body two days later. Had he been dead for two days? Highly unlikely. "John Calisto was on vacation. Did you expect to hear from him?" Ralph said.

"Yes. We expected to hear from him," Mark Jurvic said, a note of irritation in his voice. "But then, officially, he's on vacation."

"I'm not sure I understand what you mean. Can you give me a few more details?"

"Sorry, I'm not authorized to give out information other than what I just gave you."

Ralph pulled the phone away and sighed deeply. "I see. Any idea where he went on vacation?" When Mark was silent, he added, "Is there anyone there who is authorized to give me more information?"

"Just a minute. I'll see if the district attorney is free."

Another wait and more finger tapping on the steering wheel while Mark Jurvic checked with his boss. However, this proved to be an even longer wait.

"Hello, this is Charles Caliban," said a voice on the other end. "Look, sorry to keep you waiting, but I did want to speak to your chief a little further about your case."

Ralph frowned, wondering why two calls were necessary. "I understand, Mr. Caliban. Can you tell me anything about John Calisto?"

"John was working on a case involving organized crime. I think Mark mentioned that to you," Charles Caliban said, his voice heavy with concern.

"Yes, your assistant explained that."

"Okay, good. The problem is John was having trouble getting hard evidence. You understand?"

"I know all about the difficulties in finding hard evidence."

"John had been working on organized crime for some time now. Some other things came up, so we needed to pull him off that case, but he was very reluctant to do that," Caliban said. "Someone had given him a promising lead, and he wanted to follow up on it. He had vacation time coming to him, so we granted it. I couldn't argue over something he was entitled to even though it was very short notice."

"He was entitled to vacation, and he took it," Ralph said, hoping the DA would finally get to the point.

"John said he'd check in with us after the first week, but he didn't. Now he's been gone two weeks and we have no idea where he is." Charles Caliban took a deep breath before continuing. "It was brought to my attention someone found a body and you think it may be John's body? Is that right?"

"We're not sure, because we've been unable to locate the body."

"So there's still hope John isn't the victim."

"Of course. There's still hope," Ralph said gently.

"Have any idea when the murder occurred?"

"September twenty-second."

"September twenty-second?" the district attorney said. "And you're just now getting around to calling us?"

"Let me explain," Ralph said. "A woman was at the scene taking photos early one morning and stumbled across the body. There was no phone reception where she was, so she took dozens of photos for purposes of identification. On her way back to town, she met with an accident and suffered a concussion. We have reason to believe the people who murdered the victim took the digital card from this woman's camera and substituted it for another one. Whoever substituted the new digital card took photos in a different location to mislead us. The woman is older, and we thought she was confused because she suffered a concussion. We investigated the area that was displayed on the digital card but found no evidence of a murder. After she recovered and could show us where she found the body, we found the pen."

"That's why it's a probable murder," Caliban said, "There's no body. All you have is a pen to go on and an older woman's sketchy memory of what happened."

"She may be older, but I can assure you she is far from senile. In fact, her memory is quite trustworthy," Ralph said, trying to maintain an evenness to his voice. After all, John Calisto may be the DA's best friend. "We found the pen a few minutes ago, and that is the first clue we've had. Right now, I'm trying to locate the body. But we need to know who the person was, what he was doing here, and how he died. I realize this is difficult when it's one of your men. But I'd appreciate any information you can give me."

"What would you like to know?"

"I need a photo and description of John Calisto and his car," Ralph said, then added, "And any other pertinent factors under the circumstances."

"Of course, I'll send you a photo, several photos, and a physical description of John as well as his car. But I'll tell you something, you're going to have the same problem we have."

"How's that?" Ralph said.

"John had, has no family or friends. He's a loner. Works alone and lives alone."

"I see. That does make it tough. And you said he didn't check in with you while he was gone?"

"No, never called. Said he would after a week but didn't."

"I suspect you started to worry when you didn't hear from him."

"Yes, we became very concerned."

"Where was he headed?" Ralph said.

"John wouldn't discuss it before he left. Said he was on his own time while he was gone," Caliban said in a voice that suggested there was friction over the subject. "He finally agreed to call in a week's time. Since he hasn't called, we have no idea where he is."

"What about his phone? Could you locate his whereabouts by tracing his phone?"

"We issued a description of his car and got nothing. We tried tracking him through his phone, but something has happened to it because it's not emitting a signal. We have no idea where he is. I just hope he's not the man you're looking for."

"Have you listed him as a missing person?"

Charles Caliban hesitated. "No, not yet. We're giving it a little more time, then we'll call the police and ask them to list him."

Ralph ended the call and stared through the windshield. There were several unanswered questions. But the primary one was, if the DA failed to locate Calisto through his phone, why didn't he at least inform the police and give them a description of his car? Two weeks had gone by. Although, to be fair, he'd been officially missing for one week. Even so, Caliban should have notified the Cameron Police. Was Charles Caliban stalling, or was Ralph pressing too hard out of desperation? Maybe a little of both. In any case, a man was missing and there was a murder. Could they be one and the same? Without the body, there could be no identification and the murderer remained at large.

Chapter 22

"Look," Silky Voice said. "The old lady's car has to be parked some-where on the road. I'll move it behind the cabin while you continue to search, otherwise the police will start looking for it."

"You plan on comin' back ta help me?"

"No. I have other things that require my attention."

"'Require my attention'," Mike mimicked. "Like what? What could be more important than findin' that nice ole lady?"

Silky Voice turned sideways and glanced in the direction of the road. "Appointment. I have an appointment. That's what's so important."

"You got an appointment? You never said nothin' about no appoint-ment afore. What's it about?"

"My business."

"Well, seein' as you want me ta find that nice ole lady all by myself, I got a right ta know what's more important than helpin' me."

Precious seconds dissipated while both men faced off. "I have an appointment to see a doctor."

"'Bout what? You sick or somethin'?"

"No, nothing like that. I need some, uh, help with something, and he's qualified to help me."

"Help?" Mike said. Then, when a slow dawning crystalized, he continued, "You need help ta change yer face and disappear, don't ya?"

"Don't be ridiculous. It's nothing like that," Silky Voice said.

Mike studied the other man. "I don't like this whole thing one little bit."

"All right! I'll come back after I move her car. I probably should deal with something now rather than later."

Mike tilted his head. "Deal with what?'"

"Look, that nice old lady you keep talking about is an eyewitness. You know that, right?"

"Well, sure, but there's nothin' we can do 'bout it. Jist keep her here and quiet's all we can do."

Silky Voice lifted his brows. "Forever?"

"Maybe. Maybe I'd like ta keep her here forever." Mike stared off into the distance. "She looks like my granny. I don't mind one little bit takin' care of her jist like I took care of Granny."

"But she's not your old granny," Silky Voice said sharply. "Your old granny is dead."

Mike swallowed hard as his eyes narrowed. "Don't you never say that 'bout Granny! You hear me? Don't you never say that 'bout her."

Silky Voice raised his hands in defeat. "All right. I apologize. No need to get heated over it," he said. "Look. I'll move her car then come back and lend you a hand. Okay?"

"Okay," Mike said softly, but his mind drifted to what was going to happen to his granny after that.

Chapter 23

No wonder Miss Treadwell hadn't heard anyone following her for a while. There was no rush. They had the receiver. All they had to do was follow the noise she created.

For the first time, she searched her purse for the miniature microphone. The light was dim, so she used her fingertips. There it was. It almost felt like a tiny button placed in the shadow at the side near the top. She took a firm grasp, pulled it off then dug a hole in the ground beside her and buried it. As she dug the hole, she heard it repeated a short distance away, then utter silence after it was buried.

There was no telling how far away the men were. She heard nothing. They must have turned up the volume on the receiver in order for her to hear it. Was it to intimidate her? Was that their strategy? Intimidate a woman so she'd fall apart and give up? Well, she was a long way from that. She hoped.

There was a luminous dial on her watch. Eleven-thirty. Eleven-thirty! She left her house at eight-thirty. Three hours? She'd been gone three hours! Impossible. Surely someone would miss her by now. Teddy would have called to check on her and wonder where she was. Of course, if the fire was still raging on, he may be so focused on that, he wouldn't think to call.

Even so, Sam was due at her house. She would certainly contact one of the boys and a search would begin. Or had those two men done something so her two boys and Sam thought she'd left the house of her own accord and would shortly return? That could delay the search for some time. No, that didn't make sense at all. Silky Voice couldn't have anticipated she'd remember the sound of his voice and leave her house to follow him.

How many cars had she passed from the time she left the Bedford city limits until she parked her car on the berm of the road? She closed her eyes to visualize the drive mile by mile and came up with nothing. She didn't remember seeing one other car after she turned onto the backroad leading to this spot. She knew the road where her car was parked wasn't heavily traveled, but eventually someone would surely wonder why it was parked there and perhaps call the police.

Was her car parked along the same road leading to the crime scene? Or had Ralph turned off onto another road? It can be difficult to remember directions when one is the passenger rather than the driver.

She leaned back against the dirt wall. At least she was safe for now. It would be dark enough to come out of hiding in another seven hours or so. She'd crawl out of her little cave, make her way to the car and race home. Yes. All she had to do was wait it out. It was a very long wait but a safe one.

Resting, if not comfortably at least securely, she closed her eyes. Her low blood sugar was draining her of energy. Hopefully, she'd have just enough reserves to make her way through the woods to the car and drive home. Home. Hot tea. Hot bath. Comfy bed. In spite of herself, those under-appreciated reminders of home brought about a half smile.

Suddenly, Miss Treadwell's eyes opened. The sound was crushingly familiar. It was the sound of a car attempting to start, then another attempt and failure, until the engine caught hold on the third try. She knew the key was in her purse, but in her rush to enter the woods, had she forgotten to lock it? Even if she hadn't locked it, there was no extra key hidden on the outside of the car. Yet it was most certainly her ancient car. She was sure of it.

She held her breath and tilted her head. Hope faded as the car shift into gear and the sound diminished as it was driven down the road. A moment later, the sound grew ever so slightly louder. Had they parked her car near the cabin? If that was the case, there must be a path leading from the road to where the cabin was situated. Yet she didn't recall even a narrow, dirt path leading anywhere off this backroad. Obviously there was one since the van she followed from her house had disappeared at that very spot.

Suddenly, she felt utterly despondent. They'd won. Her desperate plans to escape had been foiled. Without the car parked on the side of the road, she couldn't leave. Even if she had the strength to leave, without the car in plain view, no one would ever know where she was. She shivered and drew her jacket snuggly around her. Even then, she was chilled to the bone as a depth of despair set in that she'd never experienced in her entire life.

Chapter 24

Miss Treadwell woke with a start. She searched for the clock that sat on her nightstand. Slowly, memories began to solidify within her frozen, reluctant mind. She lay her head down on the leaves, hoping nothing would crawl through her hair. Too late to worry about something as insignificant as that.

Why, why, why, she repeated to herself. Why had she been so daft as to think this was a good idea? She gambled what years she had left on finding the murderers. Now she'd be needlessly and foolishly dead.

Pressing a few leaves aside, she noted it was dark enough to leave without being seen. Her concern now was could she leave without being heard crunching through the woods? Perhaps they'd grown tired of looking for her and gone back to the cabin. She'd make her way to the road and drive home. That's when she remembered. No car. Silky Voice had moved it using some mysterious path from the road into the woods. No doubt it resided near the van—the van that delivered the chocolate candy from Bobby.

Why had Silky Voice risked being captured by the police just to deliver a box of chocolate candy from Bobby? For that's exactly what he did. She recognized his voice. For all the good it had done. Now she was cold and trapped in the woods with no escape in sight, and no one knew where she was. Any sensible person would have called the police. They would have called Ralph and let him investigate. After all this, would Silky Voice disappear, and no one would ever find him. Not only would no one find him, no one would find her either. What a fool she'd been!

Chocolate candy. Bobby. Her mind had been active even while she slept. Why would Bobby send her candy? She'd asked both boys not to call him since there was nothing he could do about it but worry. Ralph and Teddy both said they wouldn't call, and they were not in the habit of lying to her or breaking a promise. So, it begged the question, how did Bobby find out about her accident? And why would he send her chocolate candy yet not call? Didn't make any sense at all.

Having thought through that illogical piece of evidence, she moved to the next step. If that were the case, then who did send her candy? She remembered sitting down on the chair and taking the wrapper off the box of candy. She'd stopped because the voice of the man at the door belonged to Silky Voice. And if it belonged to Silky Voice then…. Her eyes widened. That was his plan to get rid of the only witness who could identify Mike's face and the voice of the man who had administered the injection that had put her conveniently to sleep.

Anger trumps a frozen mind and frozen action. Once again, she was filled with indignation and became resolute. They may have her car, but they didn't have her!

As quietly as possible, she created a hole large enough to crawl through. Drawing her purse strap over one shoulder and the camera strap over the over, she crawled several feet and stood upright. It took several tries, but eventually she stood at the top of the dip where she'd spent the entire afternoon. Which way should she turn to reach the road? Amidst the trees, and with no sun to guide her, she made an educated guess, then made her way as quietly as possible in the direction she hoped was the road. Sadly, her efforts were utterly in vain. Her footsteps sounded like a herd of elephants making their way to the watering hole.

Miss Treadwell tripped over a root and reached out to steady herself on the trunk of the tree. She froze when she heard a familiar voice say, "Careful now, ma'am. You don't wanna git hurt. You okay, ma'am? Didn't hurt yerself now, did ya?"

Sighing deeply, she said, "No, I'm quite all right. Well, I can see you've won. What do you intend to do with me? You may as well shoot me now as later."

"Oh, now, ma'am. Don't be like that. I wouldn't hurt ya," Mike said as he touched her arm. "Oh, my, my. Looky here. You're like an ice cube. Probly didn't have nothin' ta eat all day." Mike fussed over her like a mother hen. "Now, let me git ya back ta my little cabin. The fire's prob'ly down a bit, but I'll get 'er started up and you'll be nice and cozy in no time at all." Mike gently took Miss Treadwell's arm and led her slowly through the woods.

"Mike, you seem like a very reasonable person."

"Yes, ma'am. I try ta be."

"Well, in that case. I'd much prefer to go home and warm myself in my own little kitchen with a hot cup of tea."

Mike stopped and turned to her. Even in the dim light, she saw pain. "Oh, ma'am. I can't do that. Anyways, I got tea here. It's good ole black tea brung all the way from some place called Ceylon. You ever heard o' that place?"

"Oh, my, yes, Mike. That's the tea I drink at home. Well, I'd be very pleased to accept a cup of tea from you. I do hope you have milk."

"Oh, yes, ma'am. Only way ta drink tea is with milk. Sugar, too, if you want some."

"No, no. I never take sugar in my tea."

"Yep. Way too sweet. Ruins it ta pieces. Don't it?"

"Indeed, it does."

They continued through the woods with Mike lending his arm to support Miss Treadwell, who frequently tripped or stumbled in the dim light.

A recollection began to take shape as they made their way through the woods. She recalled the day of the car accident when a memory card containing all the incriminating photos of the body and surrounding area was replaced by another memory card. Miss Treadwell could not allow that to happen again. She maintained a tight grip on her camera containing photos of Mike and Silky Voice while she allowed the camera strap to slide off her shoulder. When they drew even with a tree stump, she presented a rather stellar performance of a woman about to stumble. As she neared the ground, she placed her camera on top of the stump.

Mike grabbed her arm and they continued to the clearing, the absence of the camera undetected.

When they reached the clearing, Miss Treadwell noticed the van was still there. But where was her car? Had the other man taken it, or had he moved it behind the cabin? Surely neither of them would take her car out on the road. Ralph would have the police in every county looking for it. It must be hidden in the back somewhere. The car keys in her purse were utterly useless. It would be impossible to get to it and drive away.

When Mike opened the door, the first thing she noticed was the cabin was empty. So, the other man did leave sometime earlier in the evening. That gave her a small sense of relief. At least Mike appeared kind and in no apparent hurry to dispose of her. She sighed internally. He was kind for someone who had been an accessory to murder and now held her captive. But it was far better to be at the mercy of Mike than Silky Voice.

As Mike closed the door, the warmth enfolded her. He locked the door and pocketed the key. "It ain't much, ma'am, but it's clean. Don't like nothin' that ain't clean. Even got a little bathroom through that there door," he said, nodding to the back of the room with a certain amount of pride in his voice.

"A bathroom. How lovely." Miss Treadwell sat down heavily on the nearest chair and allowed her purse to slide to the floor. She leaned back and surveyed the room before resting her head against the wall. "Yes, your cabin looks very tidy and clean. I can see we have a few things in common, Mike."

"Now, you jist sit right there, ma'am, and rest yerself. I'll have your tea ready and it'll warm you right up."

Her eyes drifted around the spare room again as Mike busied himself boiling water. Her gaze finally rested on the door, which was locked. Even if she waited until he fell asleep and, somehow, gained possession of the key, she was too weak to make her way to the road. She'd never make it. "Mike."

"Yes'um?"

"Just where is your, how shall I say, partner?"

"Uh, well, I'm not real sure 'bout that, ma'am," Mike said evasively. "Prob'ly seein' that doctor fella somewheres."

"Doctor? Is he ill?"

"Nope. Not a sick bone in his devilish ole body far as I knowed."

"I see. He didn't mention who he was going to see or where he was going?"

"No, ma'am," Mike said as he poured boiling water into a teapot. "But I got my suspicions."

It was Mike's tone of voice that both intrigued and worried Miss Treadwell. She leaned forward and said, "Just what are your suspicions, Mike?"

Mike, for all his disorderly dress and hair, was quite precise about the tea. He'd set the timer, swilled the teapot a few times, then turned to Miss Treadwell. "Now, ma'am, do you put your milk in first or last?"

In spite of her absolute fatigue and low blood sugar, she fought for control of her lips. "That's very considerate, Mike. I put milk in last."

Mike placed everything on a rough table and helped Miss Treadwell out of her chair to the table.

She waited until her entire cup of tea was consumed and felt a shadow of energy return, before repeating the question. "What are your suspicions, Mike?"

"Ooh, ma'am," Mike said, pouring her a second cup of tea before refilling his own cup. He took a sip before turning to her with a conspiratorial look in his eyes. "His face, ma'am," he whispered.

"His face?"

"I figure he gotta git that face changed, or people will knowed who he is."

Chapter 25

Ralph looked at his phone and saw Sam was calling from the lab. He stepped away from the creek, while the officers continued to comb the area for more clues. "Sam? Any news?"

"I'm afraid so, Ralph," Sam said.

"Did they deliberately try to kill her? Is that what you're trying to say?"

"Well, I'm not sure."

"What do you mean? Tell me what you found."

Sam looked at the report resting on her desk, although the results were very straightforward. "It was insulin. Whoever injected insulin into the candy made sure she'd become ill and probably create a sense of confusion in her. The problem is the dose wasn't high enough to actually cause death. Either the person miscalculated the dosage or didn't actually intend to kill her."

"I see," Ralph said, his voice tight. "But insulin can be detected.

Why use insulin and not something else?"

"As I told Teddy, your mother is old enough they may have attributed her illness and state of confusion to a stroke or any number of reasons. I tested the entire box of candy and found insulin in only one piece. There are no fingerprints on the wrapping paper or the box, so we can't trace it that way. This particular brand of chocolate candy is something easily purchased anywhere."

"Very professional," Ralph said.

"Right. He hoped her state of mind would be due to her age." She waited a few seconds, then said, "Are you all right?"

Ralph walked to the edge of the water and stared blankly upstream. "I'm all right. It's just I can't figure out why Mom left the house. She knew we were worried they'd attempt something. I just didn't think it would be something like this," he said, adding bitterly, "I was stupid. I should have planned for everything and explained to Mom all the possibilities. She would have been prepared for it. It's been hours since she left, and nobody's found her or her car. Where could she be? She couldn't have gone that far in such a short period of time. Unless...."

"Unless what, Ralph?"

"Unless she didn't leave of her own free will. They may have been in disguise when they knocked on her door, so she didn't recognize them. Maybe they persuaded her to go with them for some logical reason and took her car, so we'd think she left of her own accord," Ralph said. "But it's impossible to believe she could be deceived like that. Her mind is just too logical to be fooled by some ruse, even a well-planned ruse." He shook his head. "Although what we know so far indicates she did leave on her own. Mom's car is missing and so is her camera. But did she drop the phone accidentally or as evidence she was taken against her will? There are too many questions and not enough answers at this point."

"Don't blame yourself, Ralph. Who could have anticipated a fake call about Teddy's café catching fire or something as seemingly innocuous as a box of candy? And I agree with you. I've spent several days with her now and I can't believe she could be taken in by a disguise and fast talk." Sam hesitated a moment, "You planned for someone to be with her at all times. It's just they…."

"They outsmarted me. Apparently it's not that difficult either," Ralph said. "Look, I'm sorry, Sam. I appreciate everything you're doing. You've been great. Without you, I don't know what we'd have done."

"Don't worry, Ralph. I know you're upset. It's not directed at me. It's about your mother. The most important person in the world to you."

Ralph smiled for the first time in over two weeks. "Well, maybe not quite the most important person anymore, but a very close second."

Sam bit her lip to keep from grinning. "Thank you, Ralph. That's really nice to hear. I feel the same way."

"Do you? That's really nice to hear, too." Ralph closed his eyes. Really, he was so lame at this. He put it down to lack of experience.

"Well," Sam said. "I promised Teddy I'd call when I got the results. Hope that's all right."

"Yes, sure, he needs to know. And thanks for calling, Sam. I'll talk to you later. Okay?"

"Okay, Ralph."

Chapter 26

Cynthia Treadwell sipped her second cup of tea while she considered how to phrase what she needed to know. In the meantime, she decided to chat amicably. "I'm a bit fussy about my tea, Mike, but this is simply delicious," she said with practiced charm that rarely failed. "Where did you learn to brew tea?"

Mike blushed and smiled. "Thanks, ma'am. Granny. She learned me how 'cause she said in case she got sick I could bring her tea in the mornin'."

Miss Treadwell was nothing if not observant. There was great sorrow and pain etched in this young man's face. Whatever part he had played in this murder, there was an air of vulnerability about him. "How is your granny?" she asked hesitantly, knowing the answer.

"Well, ma'am," Mike said, clearing his throat. "She got real sick last year and, uh, well, she died."

"Oh, Mike." She reached across the rough-hewn table to take his needy hand. "I'm so dreadfully sorry. You must miss her terribly."

"I do. I miss her somethin' awful. She took me in when I didn't have nobody 'cept her."

Miss Treadwell studied the broken young man who had chosen very badly and fallen in with the wrong crowd. "How old are you, Mike?"

"Nineteen."

"So, you've been alone since you were eighteen? Is that right?"

"No, ma'am. I been takin' care o' myself since I was thirteen. My folks—well, they got themselves on the wrong side o' the law and when them people came ta git me and put me somewheres, I run away. I hitch-hiked ta Granny's house halfway 'cross the country. Never went back ta school or nothin'. When Granny got real sick, I seen to everythin'." Mike looked up. "Got me a job and paid for everythin'. I was glad ta take care o' her. Had nobody else but Granny."

"I understand." She noted the details or lack thereof as her eyes studied the room. "How long have you lived here, Mike?"

"Well." Mike leaned back and stroked his chin. "Pretty near six months, I guess. Give or take, ya understand. Not real good with dates and time. Sorta run outta money after I paid ta have Granny buried. Her pension stopped and I couldn't pay the rent with what I was makin'. 'Course I can read, and I read 'bout this here place. Been here ever since."

"Yes, I understand." She waited a moment before adding as casually as possible. "You mentioned your partner needing to change his face. Did I understand that correctly?"

"Yes, ma'am. Well, he didn't 'xactly say that. I jist figured that's what he was gonna do 'cause of that bad thing that happened." Mike looked shyly across the table. "If ya know what I mean?"

"I think so," Miss Treadwell said vaguely, wondering how murdering another human being could be considered a "bad thing". "Had you known him long?"

Mike shook his head several times before saying, "Never seen him afore that day. Nope, had no idea who that fella was until that day. Still got no idea who that fella is."

How could Mike have been a party to a murder with a partner he'd only met that day? "How did you meet this man? And how did you happen to be there?"

"Oh, I was his driver. I drove him 'round. Lost his license. Drinkin'," Mike said, with a knowing look. "I been drivin' him around over a year now."

"His driver?" Huge utterly confusing pieces were missing. It was as if Mike were talking about two completely different people and situations. He spoke of a man he'd only met very recently, yet at the same time was this man's driver for an entire year.

"Yep. Drove him everywheres. Got paid ta do somethin' I like ta do anyways. I had ta leave Granny sometimes those last six months afore I lost her. But she needed medicine and stuff," Mike said. "So, ma'am, I like it here just fine. It's away from everythin'. He give me a cell phone so he could call me, then I drove into town and picked him up."

"So, you kept his car here?"

"No, ma'am. I got a motorcycle out back. Used that ta drive ta town ta pick him up. He paid me real good, so it was worth it. Not enough ta pay rent in town and stuff. But I can buy food and such. Anyhow, I like it here real good. Private like. Nobody can see me from that there road."

"Yes, your cabin certainly is private, Mike," Miss Treadwell said, in a discouraged voice. "I don't recall ever seeing it from the road."

"No, ma'am. That there's one reason I likes it here. Can't see nothin' from the road. There's that cutout so ya can pull off the road and rest a bit or turn 'round if ya need ta. Now, inside that there cutout, if ya look real close, there's a sharp turn nobody can see, and it brings ya back ta this here cabin."

"I see," she said, offering another charming smile. "You're a very clever young man, Mike. Apparently you've thought of everything."

"Aw, well, thanks, ma'am. I done some lookin' 'round afore I settled on this here place. I wanted ta stay where Granny lived, but like I done said, when she died, I didn't have her pension money no more ta pay rent."

"Leaving the home you had with your granny must have been very difficult, Mike."

"Yes, ma'am."

"You were a driver for this man, so I'm assuming you drove to his house."

"Oh, no," Mike said, looking as if she were completely out of her mind. "Didn't never want me ta see where he lived. Didn't want me ta know his name neither, so I jist calls him Mister. You understand what I mean?"

"Yes. That was a foolish question. Of course he didn't want you to see where he lived. It would be too great a risk."

"Yes, ma'am. He was real careful about stuff like that. Always paid cash. No checks or nothin' like that. No, he parked that fancy car o' his in some big ole garage. I met him there."

"I wonder how he got there?"

Mike shrugged. "Musta took a taxi or somethin' ta the garage." He thought a moment before adding, "I only drove him ta places outta town and stuff like that. He probly took a taxi for everythin' in town," he said. "'Cept one time."

"Where did you take him?"

"He told me ta take him somewheres he coulda easy took a taxi. We pulls up ta this big, tall, fancy gate. You know the kinda gate that's all, whatcha call it, wrought iron?"

"Yes, I know what you mean. A wrought iron gate meant to keep everyone out except a selected few."

"Yeah, that kind. Well, we pulls up ta that there gate and this here fella comes outta this little hut-like place. Got a big ugly look on his face till he sees who's in the back seat. You know what he says when he sees that fella?"

"What did he say, Mike?"

"He says, 'I didn't recognize your car. I'll open the gate fer ya right away.'" Mike's memory drifted back to that day, and he was quiet as the scene played out in his mind. "I pulls up this real long driveway and come round the corner and there's this big fancy house with big fancy cars sittin' everywheres. Ya never seen so many of'em in one place. I 'member Granny telling me if it don't look right it's prob'ly not right." Mike shifted his gaze to Miss Treadwell. "It sure didn't look right, but I jist parked the car and kept my mouth shut." He took a deep breath. "And that's all I gotta say 'bout it."

The scene was puzzling, yet Mike was street smart. He was also finished discussing it, so she shifted to another topic. "I'm confused, Mike. Your partner had no license, but he took the tremendous risk of driving himself somewhere to see about his face. Wasn't he worried he'd get caught without a license?"

"Oh, well, uh." Mike stalled as he drew his brows together. "Well, ma'am, I don't know nothin' 'bout that. Maybe," he said, obviously creating a story on the fly. "He might have a license or somethin' or maybe he already talked ta somebody about his face. Don't know nothin' about it. No, ma'am," he said, shaking his head. "Don't pay ta ask too many questions."

Mike was a young man without guile, a very poor liar indeed. His stories didn't mesh. He was a driver because his partner lost his license, yet Silky Voice seemed to drive anywhere he pleased without fear of being stopped wherein his lack of license would be discovered.

She gazed at the young man who currently stared at the floor, gauging how far she could take this line of questioning before she angered him or aroused his deep suspicion. The beauty of being a bit on the elderly side of life is people rarely suspected you of anything except indigestion, sleepless nights, and arthritis. "Mike, I must ask you a very serious question."

Mike looked up, his eyes guarded for the first time, but said nothing.

"When you drove your partner here, did you know what he planned to do?"

Mike got up from his chair abruptly and moved to the stove. He checked the fire, and added two logs. "Don't want ta talk about it, ma'am. No hard feelin's or nothin' like that, but I ain't talkin' about it."

"I don't want to upset you, Mike."

"No, ma'am. I'm not upset. In fact, I was going to offer you somethin' real special."

Miss Treadwell smiled with relief. "How nice."

Mike dug something out of a drawer, placed it behind his back and approached the table with a grin, then placed it before Miss Treadwell. It was a box of chocolate candy. The first ten pieces were missing.

Chapter 27

"I love chocolate candy," Miss Treadwell said, smiling her gratitude. She reached for a piece then pulled back.

"Somethin' wrong, ma'am?" Mike said. "It's real good candy. Ate a bunch o' it myself."

"I'm sure it's delicious, Mike," she said guardedly. "Mike. Do you have the lid for this box of candy?"

Mike tilted his head but reached for it resting on a rough-hewn cupboard behind where he sat.

Miss Treadwell studied the lid and secured it onto the box. She sat back and thought while Mike watched her anxiously.

"What's the matter, ma'am? Got ta be somethin' the matter if yer turnin' down good chocolate."

"Where did you get this box of candy, Mike?"

"Get it?" Mike blinked. "Why, that fella who. I mean the man who…."

Miss Treadwell leaned forward and clasped her hands on top of the table. "Mike, did the man you were with the day I had the accident give you this chocolate candy?"

Mike's eyes dropped to the box. "Yes, ma'am. He sure did."

"Mike. Now I want you to listen to me very carefully. All right?"

"Yes, ma'am. I'm listenin'."

"The man who gave you this candy drove to my house earlier today and delivered the very same type of candy to me. He used that van he has parked outside." For emphasis, Miss Treadwell repeated the information she'd just given. "The box he gave me is exactly like this one." She allowed that to settle in before continuing, "He knocked on my door, Mike. He led me to believe it was from one of my boys living on the west coast."

"You mean the box looked 'xactly like this here one?"

"Exactly! It came covered in brown wrapping paper which is what you do if you intend to mail it through the post office or another form of delivery. Do you follow me?"

"Yes, ma'am," Mike said. Through the cloud of his constant anxiety since September twenty-second, he began to see a pattern. "He give both of us the same kinda candy," he murmured softly.

"That's right, Mike. He gave both of us the same kind of candy. Why do you think he did that?"

Mike turned sideways on his chair. His brain denied what common sense told him had to be true. Finally, he turned back, rested his elbows on the table and leaned forward. "I think he's trying to do both of us a harm."

With great effort, Miss Treadwell kept her face from displaying the relief she felt. "I'm wondering the same thing, Mike."

"But here's the thing, ma'am. I already done ate ten pieces o' that there candy and nothin' bad happened to me."

"Yes, I do see your point. But at the same time, don't you think it odd he would give both of us the same kind of chocolate candy without a reason for it?"

Mike nodded slowly. "You think he done poisoned it?"

"I'm rather worried he has, Mike. The fact that you ate some of it without ill effects is puzzling, but I do believe he intends to harm both of us."

Mike's young face twisted with indecision.

"Mike," she said gently, wondering just how far she could press the issue.

"Yes, ma'am?"

"The van parked outside your cabin. It looks just like a post office delivery van."

"Yes, ma'am. It sure does."

"What I'm wondering is this. Where did he get a van like that? Did he buy a van then have it specially painted to look like a delivery van?"

"Hm, well, ma'am, I don't rightly know," Mike said vaguely.

Miss Treadwell did not wish to press the issue and upset the young man, but she was so close to finding out a piece of critical information. "How long have you known that man? And how long has the van been here?"

Mike was silent for so long she feared she'd overstepped her boundaries with him.

"Ma'am, all I can tell ya is that there fella drove up ta my cabin here a month or so ago, maybe even two months ago, and asked if he could park that there van where you see it right now. Don't have no idea how he knowed where I lived."

"Didn't you think it an odd request?"

"Well, yes and no, ma'am. I thought it was odd till he said he'd pay me three hundred dollars a month just ta park it there, then it seemed awright. If you know what I mean?"

"Oh, yes, indeed. When one is short of cash, income is always welcomed." A thought occurred to her, and she said, "But, Mike, if he parked the van outside your cabin, someone must have picked him up."

"Oh, yes, ma'am. Somebody picked him up. For sure, somebody picked him up." Mike tapped his fingertips on the table while he worked through just how much he wanted to tell this nice lady who reminded him of Granny. "Well, it's like this, ma'am. A young lady followed him here in a regular car. Nice car. Like he had money and all." He stopped for a moment, transfixed as a memory froze his brain in place. His eyes slowly widened as he stared into space, reliving something too horrible for the human mind to grasp.

"Mike," Miss Treadwell said softly. When Mike didn't respond, she reached across the table and placed her hand on the boy's forearm. "Mike." When he turned to face her, she continued, "You were saying the man had a nice car, so he must have had money."

Unconsciously, Mike had held his breath and now exhaled and inhaled deeply. "Yep, he sure must have a pile o' money, 'cause it was a real nice car. Must have set him back a whole lot."

"What did she look like? The woman who drove the car. Did you see her?"

"Didn't see much o' her. She pulled up while I was talkin' ta this here fella then slid over ta the passenger side. Wore those big sunglasses and a hat. You know what I mean?"

"Yes. Sunglasses and a hat cover up quite a lot."

"Yep, that there's the truth. Got the feelin' she didn't want nobody ta see who she was," Mike said. "That fella settles up with me. Give me rent for two months just fer parking that van here. Six hundred dollars on the spot, ma'am! Can ya believe it? Six hundred dollars in cash!"

"A great deal of money for just parking his van here," she said with infinite patience.

"But it's like this. When he got close ta the car, she says something I couldn't make out, but he called her by name. Not real sure about the name 'cause it was a bit far away."

Miss Treadwell moistened her lips and waited until her voice was steady. "What did her name sound like?"

"Sounded like. Well, sounded somethin' like Stelle."

"Stelle," she murmured. "Surely a nickname for Stella, Estelle?"

"Might be," Mike said vaguely. He pushed the candy aside, served his homemade stew, then convinced her she'd better turn in for the night.

As she was about to drift off to sleep, she murmured, "Mike, please don't eat any more of the candy until we've had a chance to discuss it further."

"Yes, ma'am," Mike said. He covered her with a blanket, allowing his hand to rest on her shoulder. For several moments, he sat at the table staring out the window. Turning away, he picked up his knife and honed it until it reached a deadly level of sharpness then slowly carved while he thought. He smoothed out some of the rough lines of the dove he was creating, wiped it, and put it aside as his focus shifted to the candy. His mind's eye saw that man walk through the door with a bag in his hand.

"Couldn't decide what to buy so I bought one of each."

Mike waited, continuing to stare while assessing the other man's mood and motive. "Gonna tell me what ya bought?"

"Sure," the man with the silky voice said. "I bought something for you."

Ever cautious, Mike said, "Fer me? What is it?"

Silky Voice reached into a bag and handed it to Mike. "A box of chocolate candy."

He bought one of each, which means he bought two boxes of candy. So where was the other box of chocolate candy? Mike's attention shifted to the older lady sleeping restlessly on the cot. One box was for him. The other box was for the woman who reminded him of Granny.

Yet that man said he couldn't decide what to buy so he bought one of each. One of each sounds like two different kinds of candy. Yet Granny said, "The box he gave me is exactly like this one."

So, was that the plan? Put poison in the candy, thereby getting rid of the two people who could identify him? If that's the case, why had he eaten nearly half the candy with no ill effects?

Mike slept restlessly, dreaming of piles of leaves,. He awoke sharply when he thought he heard the van approaching. He got up and peered out the window. The van was where it was supposed to be. Was that movement he saw? Or was it the wind blowing objects to and fro? In the end, he decided it was the wind. Only the wind.

Chapter 28

October 5, 1995

The following morning, Mike filled the kettle with water and put it on to boil. "Won't be a minute till yer tea's ready, ma'am."

Miss Treadwell felt stiff and sore. She slowly drew her feet over the edge of the cot while she lifted her body to a sitting position. "Tea," she said softly. "I can't think of anything I'd rather have right now than tea." Her head fell forward onto her cupped hands while she allowed her mind to wake up. Out of habit, she reached for the small mirror inside her purse to check her appearance. Her eyes widened as she studied the reflection of a woman she barely knew.

"Tea's ready, ma'am," Mike said. "Made some toast, too. Hope you like toast."

"Tea and toast." She nearly purred. "That's perfect. I really can't start the day without them." She rose and made her way to the rough table and sat down as gracefully as her exhausted, aching body would allow. Closing her eyes, she sipped her first cup of tea for the day, then opened her eyes and looked across the table.

"Tea okay?"

"Delicious." Miss Treadwell smiled. "Mike?"

"Yes, ma'am," Mike said, knowing they were about to continue their conversation from the night before.

"Have you given any more thought to the chocolate candy we discussed last night?"

"Yes, ma'am. I come ta think he wants to do us both a harm 'cause we're the only ones who knows what he looks like."

"I agree with you."

Mike was quiet while Miss Treadwell sipped her tea and nibbled at her toast. She could see an internal battle raging on within this young man, and she worried which side would win. She poured another cup of tea and sipped and waited. She held her breath as he lifted his head.

"Ma'am, when you git done with yer breakfast, there's somethin' I want ta show ya."

Miss Treadwell had sipped slowly as Mike struggled, but with those words, she polished off the rest of her tea in a discouragingly short period of time. "I'm ready," she said. Out of habit, she slipped her purse over her shoulder and stood as soon as Mike headed for the door.

Mike led the way behind the cabin along a path invisible from the road. Miss Treadwell stopped short when she saw her car parked around the first bend. She glanced at the dent on the right bumper, walked the length of the car, and tried to open the door, but it was locked. "Well, well," she murmured. "It's my car, evidently I'm not permitted inside."

There were several twists and turns. At every bend in the narrow, knee-high grass, the path appeared to end. Yet as they neared the end of each stretch, there was always another sharp turn. Finally, they reached their destination. "Here it is, ma'am."

Miss Treadwell spotted a dent on the front fender. There were tiny specks of paint within the dent. She was no car expert, but the color within the dent seemed a perfect match to the color of her car. One of those men had been behind the wheel and deliberately ran her off the road. Had they intended to kill her? If so, why had they allowed her to live after she survived the accident?

She glanced in the front and backseat. The seats were covered in black leather. There were blotches of another color on the backseat, but her mind refused to consider the origin of those stains.

Even though she'd only known Mike a short period of time, she couldn't persuade herself he'd run her off the road. Yet surely there were hidden aspects of his character she knew nothing about.

She walked to the driver's side of the car, and said, "This isn't the car I photographed. Were you the one who took out my memory card and replaced it with another one? Did you take new photos, Mike?

"No, ma'am. He done all that. He took them photos. Somebody was fishing down the crick a bit, so he took photos of that there car real quiet like, so the fella didn't have no idea he was there."

"So, you don't know whose car was in the photo he took. Did you drive this car here?"

"I drove it ta this here county and parked it beside that there crick. Then I done drove it to the cabin and back to the crick agin. But that there fella drove from the crick ta this here spot after I done cleaned up that, uh, that mess."

"I'm not sure I understand what you mean, Mike."

"Well, ma'am, like I told ya, this here fella don't drive. He had a car, but he don't drive, do ya remember me tellin' you that?"

"Yes, I remember you mentioned that last night,' Miss Treadwell said. "The man owned a car but didn't drive it. His license was revoked because of a drunken driving charge."

"Yep. That's right. So, I was his driver," Mike said patiently, as if he were speaking to someone who had difficulty recalling facts.

"The man I saw seemed so very young to be able to afford a nice car and pay a driver."

"Yep, he sure was young," Mike said. "Not a whole lot older than me, I don't think."

The pieces of this puzzle refused to create a clear picture. "Do you have any idea where the money came from?"

"Well, ma'am. It's like this. He was one o' them fellas you didn't ask too many questions, if ya knows what I mean. Fact is, he told me right off. 'Don't be askin' too many questions.'"

Miss Treadwell began to visualize a situation much more complex and dangerous than a meeting gone wrong between two people. "I see," she said softly. "Did he belong to the, how shall I say, the wrong group of people?"

"Well, ma'am," Mike said, continuing to study the ground. "Some things is best ya don't know nothing 'bout," he said. "Ya git what I mean?"

Fear threatened to undermine her fragile resolve to gather information. "Yes, I'm beginning to understand." She felt it wise to leave that line of inquiry alone. "So, you were his driver."

"Yes, ma'am. He called me when he wanted ta go somewheres and I'd drive my motorcycle ta a parkin' garage where he kept this here car. I'd park my motorcycle in his spot and he'd tell me where ta take him."

"You mentioned that last night. His car was parked in a nearby town then?"

"No, ma'am. It weren't nearby. 'Bout an hour away from here. But I never took him this far afore."

"Why do you think he came here?"

Mike shook his head while he stared at the ground. "Thinkin' 'bout that ever since that day. Don't have no idea."

Mike was in a talkative frame of mind. Perhaps a cathartic mood. "What happened that day, Mike?" she said so quietly it was just above a whisper.

In a trance-like state, Mike began. "He called me that mornin', and I drove my motorcycle ta the garage. When we gits in his car, he don't give me no address. He don't tell me where we was goin' either. He just gives me the directions on where to turn and stuff. I knowed pretty quick where we was headin', 'cause I just come from there. I reckon he didn't want me ta have no written record. Figured I'd forgit," Mike said, looking up. "But I never forgit where I'm goin' or where I been."

"He must not have realized that," Miss Treadwell said.

"Yes, he must have been thinkin' 'bout somethin' else," Mike said. "Never drove him that far. Just afore we got there, he tells me ta pull over beside a crick. He gits out and tells me ta sit tight and don't move no matter what I heared or seed or nothing. Just sit tight."

"Did you see where he went?"

"Well, ma'am. He walked 'bout two hundred feet and 'round that there line of bushes. I didn't see nothin' after that."

Miss Treadwell knew exactly where he meant. She waited until her voice was under control before speaking. "You didn't see anything, but what did you hear?"

Mike's face contorted as the suppressed memories slowly rose before him. "Voices talkin', sceamin'. Couldn't hear no words. Just angry sceamin' voices. Then, then I heared some kind of strange noise, a poppin' sorta noise. And there was a different type o' screamin'. Like somebody gittin' hurt real bad type o' screamin'. I kept thinkin' maybe I oughta go see what's goin' on! Maybe help somebody or somethin'! But I remembered he said ta sit tight no matter what." Mike stopped, lost in his memories.

"What happened next?"

"He was limpin'. He was limpin' when he walked ta the car. Told me he needed ta clean up a bit. He had blood all over 'im. Seemed like there wasn't no place on him that didn't have blood." Mike moistened his lips, "So he climbed in the backseat, and I drove him here."

"After that…."

"After that, I drove him here, he got all cleaned up. He says we need ta git back and take care o'—o' somethin'. When we're jist about there, we sees that car, and we sees you and he says ta pull off the road a bit. He gits out o' the car and watches you. When he comes back to the

170

car, we wait. He says ta be quiet while he thinks." Mike relived those moments. "He tells me ta git in the back. But I don't want to git in the back cause of the stuff that's on that there seat. But he says jist sit where there ain't none of that there stuff. So I gits in the back. But it weren't easy to find a place where there weren't no blood, 'cause I couldn't sit on top o' no blood. You understand that, don't you, ma'am?"

"Oh, yes, Mike. I wouldn't be able to do that either."

Mike nodded and continued. When he sees you pull out, he follows ya. After a bit, I tell him ta be careful! You be careful 'cause you're goin' ta hit her! But he won't listen!"

Miss Treadwell stepped closer to the car and leaned against it. So that's what happened. The other man deliberately ran her off the road. She had to tell Ralph, yet she knew there was so much more Mike could tell her if only he remained in this cathartic state.

"Are you saying this man could drive but he chose not to drive? Because he did drive the car back here."

"He could drive awright," Mike said bitterly, tears filling his eyes. "I was so scared he'd git you killed. I didn't know what ta do 'cause I was so scared. I-I opened your car door and saw you wasn't dead or nothin'. So, we talked to you a bit and stuff. And later he drove me back ta that-that place next ta the crick and told me ta drive that there other car and that thing laying in the water somewheres and hide both of 'em. Blood everywheres, everywheres. I got blood on me from touchin' him. Took days ta git it off. It's still on me. I'll never git rid of it!"

"Oh, Mike," Miss Treadwell said, then remained silent as he continued.

"That fella took off. Don't know where he went or what he done. After I done what he told me, I, well, I git back to the cabin. Took me best part of an hour, but I didn't have nowheres else ta go."

"Oh, Mike," she said, knowing exactly what the boy saw. "It must have been a horrible shock for you."

"Yes, ma'am! It was a big shock awright!" Mike said. "You got no idea, ma'am. No idea."

"You have every right to be as upset as you are. I didn't realize you had no idea what was going to happen. You had no warning. You knew nothing about it."

Mike shook his head for several seconds as he breathed heavily. "No, ma'am! I didn't knowed nothin' about it. I was waitin' in the driver's seat of this here car when I heard all kinds of racket and screechin' goin' on. I was way off down the road. I heard stuff happenin' but couldn't see nothin'!" He looked at Miss Treadwell. "I didn't want ta see nothin' either. You know what I mean?"

"Yes, Mike. I know very well what you mean," Miss Treadwell said as visions of what she saw that day escaped the bolted door of her mind. "Two men met that day. Or were there more?"

Mike turned sideways and stared into the woods. "Just them two men, ma'am. I knowed that 'cause he says he has ta meet somebody. Like it was jist one person."

"Mike," she began softly. "This car belongs to the man you work for. You drove him from a garage to Muddy Creek and waited in the car while he tended to business with another man." She hesitated, before continuing, "Afterwards, you brought him back here to get cleaned up.

When you returned, you saw me taking photos, followed me and, uh, made sure I was indisposed for a time. He dropped you off at the creek to take care of the other car and the—the body. So, you hid the other car and the body, and you know where they are. Am I correct?"

Mike looked directly into Miss Treadwell's eyes. "Yes, ma'am. I knowed where the car and body is. I knowed where everythin' is, and I don't never want to see 'em agin, and nobody's never gonna find 'em neither."

Chapter 29

October 6, 1995

Ralph checked his phone to see who was calling. "Karl? Got something for me?"

"Charles Caliban, the Cameron County DA, sent some stuff marked for your attention."

"Charles Caliban. Open it and see what he sent."

There was the sound of an envelope being opened. "Well, front and profile shots. Physical description of John Calisto. Description and license number of the car he drove. Short list, very short list of names and phone numbers of people who knew him. A history of cases he's worked on in the last few years. Looks like he focused primarily on organized crime. That might be helpful. That's about it."

"Okay, good. Put it on my desk. I'll be there in twenty minutes. Thanks, Karl."

On his way back to the office, Ralph reviewed everything that had transpired the previous week. He turned off the main road and took a shortcut through the woods. Until he was nearly upon it, he didn't realize he was about to pass the scene of his mother's accident. He glanced at the tree she'd hit. If only he'd believed her at the time, they'd be a lot farther along in the case now.

He nodded at Karl and hurried to his office. The face of John Calisto was ordinary. His description fit at least ten million other men: average. Average could be a very frustrating word. The question remained, could Mom identify John Calisto from his profile photo? How much of his face was actually covered by water? Was there enough out of the water to make identification possible? And, finally, was her shock so great that her memory of his face was stripped clean?

Average. The silent hope of every police officer is a potential crime suspect with something unique enough to make identification easier. He swiveled in his chair and stared out the window as he thought about Teddy's call earlier that morning. Teddy decided it wasn't up to him to judge what was important and what wasn't.

Teddy hadn't thought sunglasses was odd at the time. Owning a café like he did, he saw all kinds of people wearing just about anything when they walked through the door. Some people didn't like making eye contact, so he didn't think too much of that either. Teddy said the man shared the same height and weight as he did and was a white male. Looked to be in his mid-thirties or so. In other words, average height, and medium build.

Teddy remembered he had a good voice. A voice that had probably spent a certain amount of time in the classroom. Smooth hands, so he probably had a desk job rather than performed manual labor. Lived in Bedford fifteen years ago, but more than likely used that as a lead-in to ask questions.

But he gave himself away when he referred to the murdered person as "he" and indicated there was more than one suspect in the case. Careless. Perhaps he wasn't the experienced criminal they were looking for. Could this possibly be the first time he'd stepped outside the boundaries of the law? Or was the man merely curious, as most people are, and they were reading too much into what he said?

Even so, could it have been the man with the silky voice Mom talked about? If that was the case, what was he doing across the street from the police station? The details from Teddy's story suggested he was fishing for how much the police knew about the case. But that was the problem. They knew very little. This case was going nowhere. They'd gotten as far as the Cameron County District Attorney's Office. After that, it was a dead end.

The phone rang and he picked it up. "Lieutenant Davies," he said crisply. While he waited for the person to speak, he noted the call was coming from somewhere in Canada. Canada?

"This is—well, I don't really want to tell you who this is, but I really do feel you should know something about the murder case you're working on. You are the person in charge of the investigation, aren't you?"

Ralph sat up straight and grabbed paper and pen. "Yes. I'm in charge of it."

"Yes. I thought so. I have some information I'd like to pass on. It's not much."

"I appreciate your call," Ralph said, gripping his pen tighter. "Please, go ahead. I'm listening." He heard the woman clear her throat and take a deep breath.

"By murder case, I mean the one involving John Calisto. The one with the Cameron County DA's office? That's the case you're working on, right?"

Ralph tried not to allow frustration and impatience to seep into his voice. "That's right. I'm in charge of the probable murder investigation. We're not sure who the victim is, but it may be John Calisto." Normally he wouldn't release that information, but he desperately needed any kind of lead he could get his hands on.

"Well, there's something I should tell you, but I wouldn't want others to find out about it. You understand what I mean, don't you?"

"Of course, happens all the time. Please, just tell me what you know."

"Well, John didn't have many friends," she said. "Actually, he didn't have any friends. But…"

"Yes, I understand he didn't have many friends. Go on."

"But he had a girlfriend that nobody knew anything about except me. Well, I don't actually know if she was his girlfriend, but they saw a good bit of each other."

Ralph dropped his pen, then picked it up again. "I'm listening."

"He kept her a secret. Didn't tell anyone about her. I suspect he didn't want her to tell anyone about him either. Just a guess, you understand."

"Right. I understand." Ralph gritted his teeth. Would she ever get to the point?

"I didn't know why it was such a big secret at the time. Sounded sort of, well, odd. But I get it now."

"Tell me why you believe he kept her a secret," Ralph said.

"It's like this. John was knee-deep working on this organized crime case and he worried they'd use her to get to him."

Ralph slowly drew his brows together. How did the caller know he was knee-deep in a case involving organized crime? "How did you find out about Calisto and the woman? Were you a neighbor or worked with one of them?"

"No," the caller said abruptly, "No, I wasn't a friend of either one of them. I just knew about them."

"I see," Ralph said. "I'm not trying to pressure you, but how did you know about them? Did you see them out together?"

"I saw them together. I live alone and sometimes I go to a little restaurant for dinner. It's an out of the way place. Quiet. I saw them together twice. The second time I happened to leave the same time they did and drove in the same direction they were going. I was going home, you see. I wasn't following them or anything like that."

Ralph raised a knowing eyebrow. "Of course not. It's not your fault if they were headed in the same direction you were going."

"Exactly. We were both heading in the same direction," she said. "John parked his car just inside an alley so you couldn't see it from the street. If you know what I mean."

"I get it. He was careful in case someone was following him."

"Right. That's it. John was being careful. And that's the first time I realized he was scared about something, so he had to protect this woman who must have been his girlfriend."

179

"This woman may have been a friend instead of a girlfriend. Is that what you're saying?"

"Well, sort of. I'm really not sure what she was to John."

"Okay." Ralph said, "Can you tell me where this alley is?"

"Uh, well, the alley is halfway down Perry Street between Center and Broad Streets."

"Are these streets in Cameron?"

"Uh, yes. They're in Cameron," she said. "John got out of his car and walked slowly to the beginning of the alley and leaned against the building. When he was sure he wasn't being followed, he got the woman and took her to the door of an apartment building there on Perry."

"Calisto didn't see you were following him?"

"Well, I, uh, I followed them without turning on my lights then pulled over and parked as soon as he pulled into the alley. I drive an old car, nothing fancy. Nothing you'd think a gangster would drive."

"So he didn't see you."

"No, he didn't see me."

Ralph held his breath as he asked the next question. "Who is she? How can I get in touch with her?"

"Can't. You can't get in touch with her."

There was something in the woman's voice that created a sense of dread within Ralph's inner being. "Why?" he said, but he knew why.

"She's dead. One more thing, Lieutenant."

Ralph rallied, and said, "What is it?"

"There's an informant in the DA's office. That's why she's dead."

Chapter 30

As soon as the words "That's why she's dead" were uttered, the woman ended the call.

Ralph looked at the notes he'd taken while the shock of what the woman said settled in. An informant in the DA's office? And that's why the woman was dead? That was always a bitter sting. One of their own turned traitor. He'd spoken to Charles Caliban, the District Attorney, and his assistant, Mark Jurvic. They both seemed straightforward, a bit worried about John Calisto, as they should be. So, they played their parts well. If theirs was an act, it was a good one.

Whoever this woman was, she recognized John Calisto at the restaurant and even knew his name. Calisto was a man who didn't have friends, yet the anonymous caller knew him, and he had a female friend no one knew about except this woman and the informant in the DA's office. Did the caller know John from the Cameron County DA's Office or somewhere else? A neighbor perhaps? Yet who was the informant, if there was one, and how did this woman know about them?

Stepping across the hallway, Ralph tapped on Chief Henderson's door. When he heard a gruff "Come in", he walked in and sat in his usual chair.

"Any new developments?" Chief Henderson said.

"A woman just called. Disguised her voice. Wouldn't give her name but added some critical pieces to the investigation."

Chief Henderson took the cigar out of his mouth and placed it on the edge of the desk. "Let's have it."

"She claims John Calisto had a female friend, possibly a girlfriend, nobody knew anything about."

Chief Henderson lifted an eyebrow. "If nobody knew anything about her, how did this woman know?"

"I wondered the same thing. Apparently this woman saw them in a restaurant twice. The second time she followed them with her car lights off."

"Ah, one of those types. Well, we need those types. Go on."

"Calisto pulled into an alley, made sure he hadn't been followed, then escorted the woman to her door."

"Calisto was investigating organized crime, wasn't he?"

"That's right."

"Hm," Chief Henderson said. "Maybe he got a little too close for comfort and didn't want her in the middle of it."

"That's what I thought. Caller said the same thing."

"Did this woman tell you where the woman lived?"

"Perry Street in Cameron," Ralph said. "Not the street number, but she gave enough information I'm sure I can find it."

"Good. I know you'll follow up on that immediately."

"There are two problems."

"What's the first one?" Chief Henderson said.

"The woman on the phone claims Calisto's friend or girlfriend is dead. Ended the call shortly after she said it."

"They always drop those bombs then walk away from them." Chief Henderson sat back in his chair, sighing heavily. "Okay. What's the second problem?"

"If what she said is true, we've really got a problem on our hands. She claims there's an informant in the Cameron County District Attorney's Office."

"An informant?" Chief Henderson said. "But how could she possibly know that?"

Ralph shrugged his shoulders. "No idea. She dropped both bombs on me in two sentences. She said, 'There's an informant in the DA's office. That's why she's dead'."

"She's suggesting someone in the DA's office is being paid off and had something to do with this woman's death? Organized crime connections? I wonder if someone from the DA's office informed the top echelon of the organized crime family and they got to the woman as a warning to Calisto."

"That's what I'm wondering, but I need to call Cameron PD and get all the details I can about the case. I won't bring up the call indicating there may be an informant in the DA's office." Ralph sat back in his chair and tapped his pen on the paper containing all the information he'd written down. "If this woman was murdered, which is what the caller suggested, you'd think we'd have heard something about this," he said slowly.

"Have any idea how long ago it happened?"

Ralph shook his head. "None. The call ended before I could ask when it happened or how she knew about the informant. I hope to find out more about the woman's death when I call the Cameron PD."

"Okay," Chief Henderson said. "Make the call. Find out what you can and get back to me."

"Yes, sir," Ralph said. When he returned to his desk, he didn't want to make the call knowing absolutely nothing, so he opened a computer file giving information about names and addresses. Within a few minutes, he found what he was looking for.

Estelle Lucca. That was the woman's name. He brought up a new page and typed in a request. She died September eighteenth. He leaves for vacation on the twentieth. Four days later, he's dead. That is, if the body they had yet to locate was that of John Calisto. There had to be a connection. Calisto's girlfriend or friend dies September eighteenth, he leaves for vacation on the twentieth, and a body is found the twenty-second. Organized crime? He read farther, leaned back in his chair, and swiveled around to look out his thinking window. No wonder they'd heard nothing about it. Estelle Lucca had died in a hit-and-run accident. Hit-and-run. No witnesses. The driver was never found.

Ralph rubbed his chin. Very convenient. The police had investigated the accident, but with no witnesses and nothing else to go on, probably attributed it to a scared driver rather than murder. Although Ralph was certain they'd considered murder as a possibility.

Even so, he called the Cameron Police Department. He identified himself, gave a few details and asked for the investigating officer.

"No leads," the investigating office said. "Working on it myself. Been two weeks now, and I've come up with nothing so far. The case is still open."

"Right," Ralph said. "Frustrating."

"You know how it is. No witnesses. At least no witnesses who would come forward," the police officer sighed. "Hit-and-run, so I considered it might be murder, but Estelle Lucca had no police record. Everything about her points to the fact that she was just what she appeared to be, a young woman who had a job, paid her own bills, kept pretty much to herself, and didn't cause any trouble."

"Was there any mention of a boyfriend?" Ralph said, still wondering if the anonymous caller knew what she was talking about. "Anything said about Estelle knowing a man called John Calisto?"

"John Calisto? He works in the DA's office. No, we don't know anything about a relationship between Calisto and the Lucca woman. And no one's come forward claiming to be a boyfriend. The neighbors said she was home nearly every night. Never saw a boyfriend hanging around. Her parents weren't sure. They hadn't met a recent boyfriend, but you know how that goes. If Estelle Lucca had a boyfriend, she may have kept it a secret for some reason. Happens all the time."

"Right, I know." Ralph closed his eyes.

"Except," the police officer said. "It was kind of strange, in a way."

"Oh?" Ralph said, trying to tamp down this feeling of hope.

"Estelle Lucca's immediate family had a clean record. No arrests, steady jobs, not overloaded with debt." The police officer hesitated. "I considered it at the time, even though it's a very thin line of inquiry."

"I understand. Tell me what you think," Ralph said.

"Estelle Lucca came from a good family. No history that would tie her to a contracted hit-and-run incident." The officer hesitated again. "But during the investigation, I ran across Antonio Lucca, a distant cousin, who had connections to organized crime. He personally has no police record, but there's no doubt he's very friendly with a branch of the Lucca family who is involved."

Ralph sat up abruptly in his chair. "Were you able to question him?"

"Huh!" the police officer said. "By the time I found out about him, he'd left the country."

"I see."

"Worse yet, he doesn't have to come back."

"How's that?" Ralph said.

"Antonio Lucca has dual citizenship, so he can stay away for the rest of his life if he wants to."

Ralph asked a few more pointed questions, thanked him, and ended the call. It was disappointing to think he had a lead, only to discover the lead had left the country. He needed time to think and discuss this with the Chief. Yet, this was the first connection between the organized crime unit and John Calisto's personal life. Antonio Lucca. Same last name as Estelle. Antonio was a distant cousin. Friendly with the wrong people but no police record.

There had to be other relatives in that distant cousin's family. Then again, the police officer at Cameron PD would have thought the same thing and pursued that line of inquiry. Beyond that, there may be no connection between Estelle Lucca's death and her distant cousin, Antonio Lucca. And yet. Hit-and-run. He stared out the window unseeing.

Chapter 31

Ralph made a phone call, then got in his car, and headed for the interstate where he'd turn south towards Cameron County and the home of Estelle Lucca's parents. Enough time had passed since the hit-and-run accident that a memory may have surfaced they'd forgotten in the initial shock of their daughter's death.

As he drove, he allowed his mind to drift in a different direction.

Where was his mother? Was she still alive? Had she been captured and was now a prisoner of those two men? The anxiety never left him.

Ralph's mind drifted farther back to the time he was five years old. He remembered the day the police knocked on the door of his house. The neighbor girl was caring for him, and she opened the door. The police asked her to find something for him to do in another room. When she returned, the officer explained Ralph's parents had been killed in an accident. The girl covered her face and sobbed. Not so much from grief as shock. No, she didn't think there were any other relatives, so social services got involved and soon discovered the girl had been correct. The little boy was utterly alone in the world.

Even now, Ralph remembered sitting silently on a chair at the large, rambling social services building while the woman studied him over her halfmoon glasses.

"Ralph," the woman began kindly. "I know a very nice lady who would be delighted for you to live with her."

Ralph said nothing. He hadn't spoken a word since the police told him what happened. Not even a syllable. The woman took him to her car, drove across town, and down a long driveway lined with cottages. The car stopped at the last cottage. The woman led him to the house where Cynthia Treadwell was housemother.

Miss Treadwell dropped to her knees. She smiled into the little boy's lonely, frightened eyes and told him she would do her best to make him feel safe and happy. Ralph's mind was frozen, so he didn't think in terms of happy or sad or even safe.

She rose from her knees, gently took his hand, and led him to a rocking chair in her small sitting room away from the other boys where it was quiet. She gathered him onto her lap and rocked while pressing his ear against her chest. She hummed. The soothing humming sound transferred to his ear and reverberated throughout his little body. She rocked and hummed for an hour.

At the end of the hour, Miss Treadwell studied the little boy whose eyes were vacant. She decided to prepare a little cot at the far end of her bedroom. He wasn't ready to join the other boys yet.

Every day for four weeks, she rocked the little boy and hummed. At the end of that hour, she'd peer into his eyes and say, "I love to rock. Don't you, Ralph?" Ralph stared into space and said nothing.

Eight thirty was bedtime. After tucking him in his cot, she smoothed back his hair and told him she loved him.

At the end of that month, he spoke for the first time. When Miss Treadwell said, "I love to rock. Don't you, Ralph?" The little boy said one word: "Yes."

Miss Treadwell's eyes misted over, and she held the little boy close to her. That night when she tucked him into his cot and told him she loved him, he looked at her for the first time and said, "I love you, too."

Miss Treadwell pressed her trembling lips into a smile.

Ralph thought for a moment, and said, "Are you going to be my mommy?"

She gathered him into her arms. "Yes, dear. I'm your mommy."

By the following week, Ralph decided, on his own, that he would like to join the other boys upstairs at bedtime. And, on his own, he chose to join Teddy and Bobby in their room.

The three boys grew up together sharing the same room: Ralph, Teddy, and Bobby. They played, wrestled, and competed with each other as boys will.

At Teddy's seventeenth birthday party, they stuffed themselves with cake and ice cream then drifted through the front door and sat on the bottom step of the house. Teddy was unusually quiet for a boy celebrating his birthday. He pulled a blade of grass from the yard and tore it apart a half inch at a time while his eyes searched the future.

Eventually, his worries spilled out. "You know what happens when we turn eighteen, right?"

The other two boys knew but remained silent. "This time next year, the superintendent is going to kick me out of here. I'll be on my own, and I don't have any idea what I'm going to do."

Their housemother stood at the screen door, ready to join the boys but stopped from pressing through when she heard Teddy's remark. She was familiar with the regulation. Young people who go to college, trade school, or join the armed forces at least had a place to live and some direction in their lives. They had time to mature. These boys would be cast out rudderless.

Instead of joining the boys, she walked to her small sitting room at the back of the house. Two hours later, the boys tapped on her door, kissed her goodnight, and headed quietly up the steps. After they left, Miss Treadwell continued to analyze the problem. That fall, she would turn fifty-nine and could take early retirement. She'd planned to buy a cottage in the country. But a larger house would do just as nicely. Her mind settled, she prepared to turn in for the night.

A month later, she asked the three boys to join her in her sitting room because she had something to tell them. She had bought a house just outside of Bedford. It was large enough for all four of them. She'd already cleared it with the administration at the group home for boys and they were moving in two weeks. They would always have a home with her for as long as they wanted to.

The three boys were speechless for five seconds. They pounded each other on the shoulder while brushing the back of their hands across their eyes.

Ralph smiled as he remembered that day. He took the Cameron exit off the interstate, made the last two turns, and stopped in front of a house.

Chapter 32

The woman who answered had died with her daughter. Mrs. Lucca was merely going through the motions of being alive.

"Yes?"

Ralph presented his identification. "I'm Detective Lieutenant Ralph Davies from the Bedford Police Department. I called earlier."

"Of course." Mrs. Lucca opened the door and led him into a room where a man sat looking out the window. "Mario. It's the police officer from Bedford."

Mr. Lucca rose to his feet and shook hands out of habit.

"I know this is a difficult time for you. If it weren't important, I wouldn't have come."

Mr. Lucca indicated a chair for Ralph, then took his wife's arm and led her to the sofa where they sat shoulder to shoulder holding hands. Tragedy had bonded them.

"I'm sorry for your loss. I realize talking about Estelle will always be painful, but what can you tell me about her?"

Mr. Lucca cleared his throat and dabbed his eyes. "She was a good daughter. Our only child. Good student in school. Had lots of friends. Had a good job, so she didn't need any help from us. She only lives... She only lived a mile away. We're getting on a bit, and she didn't want to live too far from us. You know what I mean?"

"Of course. I feel the same way about my mother," Ralph said, feeling a catch in his voice.

"You're a good son," Mrs. Lucca said.

"Thank you," Ralph said. If he were such a good son, his mother wouldn't be missing right now. "Was Estelle seeing anyone in particular?"

"She had dinner a number of times with a man. We didn't really think it was serious because she never brought him home for us to meet," Mrs. Lucca said.

"Did you think it was strange you didn't meet this man?"

"Yes, we thought it was odd," Mrs. Lucca said. "It's not that we asked to see them. Estelle just brought them around."

"Do you know anything about this new man?"

"Very little," Mr. Lucca began. "He must have had a good job because he took her to nice places. Out of town restaurants mostly."

"Did you see Estelle often?"

"Twice a week. Came for dinner Wednesday and Sunday nights. Always called us those afternoons to tell us she'd be here on time," Mr. Lucca said. "Never missed until the Wednesday night before the accident."

"Had you talked to Estelle the Wednesday afternoon before the accident and had she indicated she was coming?"

"Oh, yes," Mr. Lucca said. "She called early that afternoon to say she wouldn't be late for dinner. Then a couple of hours later, she called back to say she couldn't make it after all."

"Did she tell you why she wouldn't be here for dinner that night?"

"She said something had come up," Mr. Lucca said. "This fellow was delivering a van somewhere and needed someone to follow him and drive him back to town."

"She said she was the only one who could do that," Mrs. Lucca said. "We asked her about it, but he didn't want her to tell anyone."

Ralph dropped his eyes, trying to maintain control. "Did she mention a name?"

"No," Mr. Lucca said. "She wouldn't say."

Why would a good daughter keep a secret about something as seemingly innocuous as that? "Did Estelle mention where they went or which direction they'd take?"

"Somewhere north is all she told us," Mrs. Lucca said.

Bedford was the next county north of Cameron. "Estelle didn't show up for dinner that Wednesday. How many days later was the accident?"

"Three days," Mrs. Lucca said.

"Did the police see any connection between Estelle following this man in his car and the accident?"

"Connection?" Mr. Lucca said. "I don't think there's a connection. Do you, Sophia?"

"No. Estelle wore dark clothes, and the driver just didn't see her. The police said it was an accident, so it didn't even cross our minds to bring it up," Mrs. Lucca said. "But there was another man who stopped by. He asked more questions than the first police officer did."

Ralph looked up sharply. "What other man?"

"He called. Said he was with the authorities investigating the accident and asked if he could stop by. That's when it came up about her missing Wednesday night," Mrs. Lucca said.

"He asked if she missed dinner that night because she had to follow someone to Bedford County and bring him back. We were surprised he asked, weren't we, Sophia?"

"Yes," Mrs. Lucca said softly. "But now that I think about it, how did he know she followed that man up north in order to bring him back to Cameron? We never mentioned it to the first police officer. We didn't even know it was Bedford County, so how did he?"

"And he was from the police department?"

"He didn't show us any identification. We just assumed he was," Mrs. Lucca said.

"Do you remember his name?"

"Jurvic," Mrs. Lucca said. "I think his name was Jurvic."

Not a common name. What were the chances? "Do you remember his first name?"

The couple exchanged a few words, then turned to him. "Mark," Mrs. Lucca said. "We think it was Mark Jurvic."

"What did Mark Jurvic look like?"

"About as tall as you," Mr. Lucca said.

"Six feet two inches then. That's how tall I am."

"That sounds right. Big fellow. Much larger than you. Probably weighed well over two hundred pounds."

"When Mark Jurvic mentioned your daughter followed a man to Bedford county in order to help him deliver a van, did he say anything else about it?"

"Didn't say anything else, did he, Mario?" Mrs. Lucca said.

"No, but it was then we remembered we hadn't told the other policeman and asked him if we should have," Mr. Lucca said.

"And what did Mark Jurvic say about it?"

"He said not to worry. That they found out about it during the investigation," Mr. Lucca said. "He said he was just verifying it."

"Mark Jurvic said the police discovered Estelle was helping a friend deliver a van to Bedford County on that Wednesday."

"Yes," Mr. Lucca said. "That's what he said. The police found out about it and that's how he knew."

"Did he say how they found out about it?"

"No," Mrs. Lucca said. "I suppose we should have asked, but we didn't."

Ralph had saved the question concerning Antonio Lucca till the end. "I just have one more question," he said, observing the look of relief suddenly leave their faces. "Antonio Lucca. I believe he's a distant relative of yours, Mr. Lucca?"

"Oh, well," Mario Lucca said. "Antonio's father is my cousin, so I consider Antonio to be a distant cousin."

"When someone is born in one country then moves to another country and gains citizenship, some countries allow dual citizenship. Do you know whether Antonio's family has dual citizenship?"

"Now that you mention it, I believe they do," Mr. Lucca said.

"So, Antonio Lucca has dual citizenship. Is that right?"

"That's my understanding. Antonio was a little older than Estelle. We met him a few times at reunions but didn't know him very well."

"Did Mark Jurvic ask you about Antonio Lucca?"

"Why, uh, I believe he did," Mr. Lucca said.

"Do you remember what questions he asked you?"

Mr. Lucca shook his head. "I don't remember what he asked about Antonio. We were still in shock. We still are."

"You've been extremely helpful. Thank you very much." Ralph handed them his card and let himself out of the house. He sat in his car studying his notes. What was there about John Calisto she didn't want her parents to know? And why did they seem uncomfortable when he mentioned Antonio Lucca?

Ralph knew John Calisto was the man Estelle helped deliver the van. But it didn't make sense that the hit-and-run was contracted solely because she helped a man deliver a van from Cameron County to somewhere in Bedford County, unless there was more to it than that.

If the anonymous woman on the phone were to be believed, Estelle's death was because someone inside the DA's office was an informant. Was she murdered because someone was worried Calisto had told her more than he should have, so they contracted to have her killed then eliminated him several days later at Muddy Creek?

Mark Jurvic, the assistant to the DA, knew about this and never said a word to his boss, the district attorney. But if he had, the DA deliberately withheld the information during their phone conversation. Both men had withheld information.

As Ralph pulled away, Sophia Lucca turned to her husband. "Should we have told him, Mario?"

"No, can't tell anyone. That's the last thing he said. Don't tell anyone."

Chapter 33

As Ralph pulled onto the interstate highway leading north to Bedford, he reviewed what Mr. and Mrs. Lucca said during the interview.

Calisto had been meticulously careful in protecting his relationship with Estelle Lucca. Yet with all the care he took, she had been murdered. That's how Ralph viewed Estelle's death. Murder.

Ralph understood why Estelle's parents saw no connection between the secret boyfriend, the unknown destination of the van, and her death. But Mark Jurvic had been curious enough to make a special trip to the Lucca's' house to discuss it. Why had he led them to believe he was from the police department?

As he walked down the hallway to his office, the missing pieces dominated his thinking. Start with the source was his final decision, and he punched in the number for the Cameron County DA's office.

"District Attorney's Office, Mark Jurvic speaking."

"This is Lieutenant Ralph Davies of the Bedford PD. I spoke to you recently regarding a pen we found near Muddy Creek, the possible scene of a murder."

There was a slight hesitation. Was the hesitation because he was searching his memory for the jist of their previous phone conversation, or was he arming his rebuttal for any questions that may arise?

"Oh, yes, Lieutenant. What can I do for you?"

"There was a hit-and-run incident in Cameron on September eighteenth killing Estelle Lucca. Do you know anything about that?"

"Yes, the investigating officer briefed us on that, but there's not much to go on."

"I thought you should know I interviewed Mr. and Mrs. Lucca this morning."

"How did it go?" Jurvic said, in a disinterested voice.

"As well as can be expected in a situation like that." Ralph hedged. "They mentioned something about Estelle helping a male acquaintance deliver a van to an area north of town just three days prior to the hit-and-run accident. They said the male acquaintance wanted his name and the destination kept strictly confidential."

Jurvic interrupted, "Don't you think you should be having this conversation with the investigating officer?"

"I did discuss the case with the investigating officer and that subject never arose. It may prove to be a critical piece of evidence in the case, and it's difficult for me to believe he would leave that fact out of our conversation."

"Delivering a van somewhere is hardly relevant. That's a very ordinary thing to do in the broad scheme of things."

"I agree," Ralph said, swiveling his chair around to look out his window. "But Estelle always introduced a new boyfriend to her parents, without fail. Why did she keep this new boyfriend a secret, especially when she called off their scheduled Wednesday night dinner to help him deliver a van somewhere? And why did the boyfriend tell her not to reveal the destination of the van delivery? Those don't seem ordinary."

"You know how young people are. Doesn't sound like it amounts to anything in my opinion."

After their conversation ended, Ralph sat with chin resting in his cupped hand. His phone buzzed and he noted the call was coming from someone in Canada again. Ralph sat up and grabbed his pen. "Lieutenant Davies," he said, striving for calmness.

"I thought you should know something." It was the same woman who had called earlier.

"I'm listening," Ralph said.

"It's probably nothing, but I think you should know John Calisto was diabetic."

"Diabetic?"

"Yes, he'd suffered from it for quite some time," she said. "Always had to test himself to make sure his sugar wasn't too high or low. If you know what I mean?"

"Of course, I understand what you mean."

"Like I said, it's probably nothing, but a couple of times he wasn't any too careful and ended up in the hospital. They had to adjust his insulin."

Ralph sat bolt upright. "Insulin you say. John Calisto was a diabetic on insulin, so he carried it with him."

"Oh, yes. I'm sure he took enough with him to last the two weeks he was supposed to be gone."

"I take it you knew John Calisto fairly well then."

"Well, not really, just knew a few things about him. That's all. I sort of looked out for him."

"Was he a good friend? Perhaps a boyfriend?"

"No, no, nothing like that. I just knew who he was."

"It would be nice to call you by name."

"Oh, no, too dangerous to do that," she said and ended the call.

Insulin. John Calisto was diabetic and carried a good supply of insulin with him. And insulin was injected into his mother's chocolate candy. But not enough to kill her, Sam had said. He made a quick call to Sam at work. She had worked the night shift but had stayed on to help clear up the backlog. She'd take a break, meet him at the café in thirty minutes then return to work. Ralph crossed the hall, tapped on Chief Henderson's door, and brought him up to date.

Ralph chewed on a French fry while Teddy and Sam studied his weary face.

"Anything new?" Teddy said.

"Several things, but I got a call from someone informing me that John Calisto was diabetic."

Sam was the first to make the connection. "Insulin," she whispered.

"That's how insulin got into the candy someone sent Mom," Teddy said. "Whoever murdered Calisto rummaged through his luggage and took his insulin. But why would anyone do that unless he planned to harm someone? I mean, Calisto was already dead. How could the killer know there were others he wanted to take out?" Teddy said. "I thought insulin had to be refrigerated."

"It's good for four weeks if it's kept relatively cool," Sam said. "I wondered the same thing. Why would the killer take the time to go through John Calisto's possessions and take out the insulin?"

Ralph studied the design on the table while Teddy and Sam sipped their coffee and waited. "This doesn't make sense unless they are hiding nearby."

"How do you figure?" Teddy said.

"Mom was in that area for some time taking photos. The body was on the other side of that line of bushes the entire time. We have no idea when the murder occurred, because anyone passing by on the road probably saw a car but not the body underneath it. For whatever reason, whoever killed Calisto left for a time then returned to clean up the mess."

Sam leaned forward. "In the meantime, your mother found the body, shot the photos, left in her car, had the accident and was drugged by the killer."

"Right," Ralph said. "We thoroughly searched the surrounding area where Mom shot the photos and can't find Calisto's body or his car. A possible explanation is the killer put the body back into the car, drove some distance and deposited the car and body in a place that is well hidden."

"And his accomplice drove behind him in a separate car to pick him up," Teddy said. "Since they laced Mom's candy with insulin, you figure they may still be around, or do you think they would have left the area?"

"I suspect they stayed long enough to know whether Mom ate the candy," Ralph said.

"And the man who was here asking me a lot of questions may have been one of them," Teddy said.

"I know. I've thought the same thing," Ralph said, sighing heavily. "The question is, where's Mom? I know they have her somewhere. We just don't know where, or…."

"Or if she's still alive," Teddy added softly.

Ralph looked over their heads for a moment while he sifted through a new thought. "What if," he began. "What if Mom was injected with insulin the day of her accident?"

'You mean the day John Calisto was killed and she found the body," Teddy said.

"Right," Ralph said. "The injection of insulin wasn't enough to kill her, just enough for her to lose consciousness. Between the insulin and the concussion, her thinking would be muddled, confused. I think that's what he was aiming for. An unreliable witness."

"But do you think the killer would take time to search through Calisto's suitcase before he moved the body?" Sam said. "I think he'd wait until he had the body out of sight."

Ralph shook his head. He gazed through the café window as the sun reflected off the roof of the police station across the street.

Again, Teddy and Sam sipped their coffee in silence and waited. Finally, Ralph turned to them with a questioning look on his face. "I may have been wrong about everything. And if that's the case, we're going to have to start from the very beginning."

"What do you mean?" Sam said.

"Why did they push Mom's car off the road at that exact spot?" Ralph said. "Why not earlier or later? Was there a reason they chose that spot or was it random? It looks like just a cutout in the road, a place to turn around. But what if there is an access that leads farther into the woods that is invisible from the road?" His eyes rested on the remains of his food as another thought took shape. Suddenly, he stood. "I should have thought of that," he murmured. "I need to make a phone call. Catch up with you later."

Ralph burst though the police station door, trotted back to his office, and closed the door. He punched in the phone number and tapped the tips of his fingers impatiently on his desk until his call was answered. "Jeb, it's Ralph. Look I need a favor. A big one. And I need the favor right now while I'm on the phone."

Chapter 34

With one last sober look at his employer's car, Mike walked slowly back to the cabin with his head down and his hands stuffed deeply into his pockets.

Miss Treadwell trailed along behind him dividing her attention between Mike and the surrounding area. The trees and undergrowth were largely impenetrable for a vehicle, yet there was the occasional open area. But were they wide enough for a car to drive through without leaving visible damage to the sides of the trees? She couldn't detect damage from this distance. There weren't parallel lines in the tall, straggly grass indicative of car tracks. But the grass would have had time to recover, so the fact that the grass was relatively level was not important.

Could she risk walking closer to the open areas without drawing attention to it? Mike said he had taken the murdered man's car and body to a place no one would ever find. Would he have chosen a place this close to the cabin to hide the car and body? Only a closer examination of the trees would settle that question, and she drifted nearer to an opening.

Mike stopped and turned. "Yer laggin' behind, ma'am. You tired?" he said, his eyes studying her face for signs of fatigue.

"Oh, no, I'm fine. Just admiring the beauty of nature."

"You think it's perdy?" Mike said, looking around as if he'd seen it for the first time. "Feels more like a prison to me, ma'am."

Miss Treadwell shielded her eyes with her hand as she looked up at the young man in surprise. "A prison? Why do you say that?"

Mike shrugged, shifting his gaze back to the ground as he ambled along. "Can't leave. Can't go nowheres. Can't go nowheres in a prison neither."

"You have your motorcycle. Surely you can use that to leave."

"No, ma'am. He done took the keys ta it."

"You mean the man who is your, how shall I say, your partner took the keys to your motorcycle?"

"Yes, ma'am. He sure did."

Remembering how Silky Voice started her car even though he had no keys, she said, "Can't you override the system? Can't you start the motorcycle without keys?"

"Yep, but he done took the spark plug connector and that's why I can't leave."

Having no idea what a spark plug connector was, she said, "But there's the van, and my car is just behind the cabin." She glanced at Mike to determine how receptive he was to that suggestion. "I have the keys to my car, and we could certainly use those to leave."

Mike said nothing for a discouraging length of time. "No hard feelins', ma'am. But that jist won't work. We'd be picked up in no time, and I'd end up in a real prison."

"But Mike."

"Sorry, ma'am. Don't mean no rudeness or nothin' like that, but that's jist how it is."

"Won't you run out of food supplies soon?"

"I'm set for another week or so," Mike said. "That fella done bought a bunch o' stuff last time he went ta some town 'round here."

"He risked going into town?"

"Wasn't much of a risk, ma'am," Mike said. "He had this ole cap pulled way down over his face, and he hunched over a bit. Least that's what he done told me. He never went ta the same place twice. Weird. I'm tellin' ya, he is one weird fella."

She reviewed the small towns within a thirty-minute drive from here. There were several, but surely a stranger would be noticed. A stranger may be noticed, but most probably he'd be very difficult to describe and easily forgotten as soon as he left.

Mike held the cabin door open, and Miss Treadwell glanced at the van, wondering if the keys were hidden somewhere inside or if the spark plug connector had been removed from that as well. The employer's car, her car, the van, and Mike's motorcycle were within a few steps of the cabin, yet she was trapped. Sighing under her breath, she slipped through the door, then waited for the discouraging sound of the key turning in the lock which came seconds later.

"Want to see all the stuff I been workin' on?"

Miss Treadwell rallied and smiled. "Of course, Mike. I'd love to see them."

Mike strode purposefully to the chest behind the table and opened a drawer. "I keep 'em in here." He brought out all his carved objects and placed them on the table.

There was the owl, the fox, and the eagle. Then her eyes rested on the partially finished dove. The dove. The eternal symbol of peace. If only….

"They're lovely, Mike. You have a gift for carving," she said, attempting to keep the surprise out of her voice. "Where did you learn to carve like this?"

"I done learned all by myself. Been doin' this since I was a kid," Mike said. "Granny bought me a knife and a sharpener and a chunk o' wood. She give me 'nother new knife ever' year since I was twelve." He opened the drawer again and said with boyish delight, "Wanna see 'em?"

"I'd love to." Miss Treadwell joined Mike in front of the opened drawer. Her eyes traveled along the lovingly maintained knives. "You've certainly taken good care of them."

"Yep, keep 'em nice and sharp 'cause you never knowed when you might need 'em for somethin'. Thinkin' 'bout hidin 'em, too."

Miss Treadwell wasn't quite sure what he meant by that, but suddenly she needed to sit down rather quickly. She steadied herself on the edge of the table, worked her way around to the other side, and sat down at what had become her usual spot. Once again, she rallied her courage. "Why would you need to hide them?"

"'Cause one of 'em is missin' and I don't wanna lose no more."

Lovingly, Mike returned his carved animals to their padded home inside the drawer and sat down. "You 'member me tellin' you 'bout the day that guy brought up that there van ta park behind the cabin? That Stelle woman drove behind him and waited till we finished business, and they left. You 'member that?"

"Oh, yes. You mentioned he paid you cash."

"Yep, he sure did. He come into my cabin. Said he forgot ta put a set o' keys under the mat in the van and would I go do that fer him." He shifted in his chair as he relived that day. "I think he done that ta check out my place. He opened that there drawer and seen my knives."

"How do you know that?"

"'Cause when I come back, he was standin' there studyin 'em."

"The missing knife, Mike? Did he take it?" she said softly.

"Sure did," Mike said between gritted teeth.

Miss Treadwell's heart beat faster. "Did he take it the day he brought the van here or later?"

Mike turned his head and stared at Miss Treadwell. "It went missin' the day we was lookin' for ya in the woods. He musta come in here after he brung your car from the road ta behind this here cabin. And I knowed why he done took it, too."

"Why did he take it?"

"'Cause he figured he'd be needin' it."

Miss Treadwell sat stunned into silence. Suddenly, nothing made sense. She started to speak but realized she was too confused to ask a question. She needed to buy herself time to think. "Mike," she began absently. "Would it be too much trouble to brew another cup of tea?"

Mike jumped up, seemingly relieved to have something to do to take his mind off where it had stagnated. "No, ma'am. Be glad ta git it fer ya."

While he brewed the tea, she reviewed the facts. The man who parked his van here was the same man who delivered candy to her house and gave an identical box to Mike as well. This was no act of generosity. It was a calculated means of eliminating two witnesses.

Then a terrifying thought struck her. All the vehicles were accounted for: the employer's car, the van, her car, and the motorcycle. Yet the man with the silky voice was missing. He'd been here the afternoon of October fourth when she took photos of the two men arguing. But that was two days ago. So, if all the vehicles were within easy reach of this door, where had he gone and why had he taken the knife?

Chapter 35

Ralph walked across the hall to the Chief's office and tapped on the door.

"Come in," Chief Henderson barked. "You looked harried, Ralph. What's on your mind?"

Ralph sat forward in his chair. "Chief, I've been thinking about the spot where Miss Treadwell had the accident. It looks like a simple cutout on the side of the road. But what if it isn't? What if the killer, or killers, deliberately chose that spot to edge her car off the road? What if there's a path that goes deeper into the woods that isn't obvious unless you know it's there?"

Chief Henderson slowly nodded his head. "We should have thought of that. Take some officers out there and have a look around."

"Yes, sir." Ralph stood and headed quickly for the door.

"Ralph," Chief Henderson said. When Ralph turned, he added, "Be careful. They have nothing to lose."

"Yes, sir."

Ralph called a short meeting and explained his theory and how they would proceed to each of the seven officers. Within forty-five minutes of his conversation with Teddy and Sam, four patrol cars slipped quietly out of town.

When they reached the last bend in the road before the cutout, Ralph instructed Karl to pull over. All the officers followed Ralph as he rounded the bend on foot. They could see the edge of the cutout from where they stood.

After a few last-minute instructions, Ralph said in a low voice, "Don't take any chances and keep within visual contact of each other." They spread out and entered the woods within a few yards of where Cynthia Treadwell had just two days earlier.

Miss Treadwell stirred her tea as she thought through the various possibilities. Unless there was a vehicle she knew nothing about, Silky Voice must have left on foot. Either that or—and she swallowed hard at the following possibility—he never left. The last thought was so chilling she laid down her spoon and, with a hand that shook ever so slightly, sipped her tea.

Noting her silence, Mike said, "Ya awright, ma'am?"

"I'm fine, Mike." She drew from her inner resources and said, "I'm confused."

"'Bout what, ma'am?"

"I'm confused about how your partner left here when all the vehicles appear to be accounted for. There's your employer's car, your motorcycle, the delivery van, and my car." Miss Treadwell took a shallow breath. A deep breath always suggests anxiety on some level. "I'm wondering if you can help clear up this confusion."

Mike dropped his head and studied his hands while his mind drifted back to the days sitting at Granny's kitchen table while they chatted. His mind moved through the process of Granny's eventual decline till bedrest was the only option. He prepared her tea and meals on a tray, then sat nearby watching her slowly lift her shaking fork or teacup to her lips. He refused to allow his mind to visualize that last day with Granny. He looked up and said, with a faraway look in his eyes, "I got somethin' else to tell ya and somethin' else to show ya if yer willin'."

Fearing the worst, she said, "I'd like to hear what you have to say and see what it is you'd like to show me."

Mike came around the table and gently took her arm as Miss Treadwell rose to her feet, drawing her purse over her shoulder. "Now, you be real careful, Granny. Don't want you fallin' or nothin'."

Miss Treadwell froze for a second but recovered quickly. "Thank you. I confess I am a bit shaky." She allowed him to slowly lead her through the door and around to the back of the cabin. Eventually, they reached his employer's car and entered the woods a moment later.

"Ya ain't gettin' too tired are ya, Granny? Don't want ya gettin' sick again over this."

"Oh, no, dear," Miss Treadwell said with a fluttering voice she hoped was reminiscent of his grandmother. "I'm doing quite well."

They stepped over fallen limbs and detoured to take an easier route while Mike slowed his pace and frequently checked her for signs of exhaustion.

Miss Treadwell found it relatively easy to assume the character of Mike's granny, for she was exhausted. She was now functioning on reserves she thought impossible and wasn't at all sure she could maintain her poise. She frequently glanced at Mike, wondering how long this mental aberration would continue. When they arrived at their destination, would his mind revert and realize he'd just given the game away? Until now, Mike had shown her nothing but kindness and goodwill because she was no discernable threat and she reminded him of his grandmother. Once they arrived, would he suddenly realize his disastrous error, and have to deal with the consequences.

Mike's delusion may last only a few more moments. "You said you wanted to tell me something. I'm ready to listen now."

"Now, I don't want ya gettin' upset with me," Mike said as he searched her face. But all he saw was affection and curiosity. He took a deep breath and began. "You 'member the other night when we was lookin' for ya in the woods?" When his granny nodded, he continued. "After a bit, that fella went out ta the road and done somethin' ta git your car started, and I heared him pull it 'round back ta the cabin. Then I gets to thinkin' maybe I'd better go make sure he weren't gonna take off or nothin' like that 'cause I didn't know how I was ever gonna find you by myself."

Mike stopped walking and turned to his granny, but her expression hadn't changed. "So, I walked back to the cabin, but he weren't nowheres I could see." He replayed the scene in his mind, then continued, "He weren't in the front or side of the cabin, so I walked 'round back and seen where he parked yer car. The van was still there, so there was only one other place he could be. I found him inside the cabin. And—and…."

"And what, Mike?"

"He's in front of that there cupboard where I keep the knives you give me. He done picked up one and he was lookin' at the others. He didn't hear me walk in 'cause the door weren't all the way closed. When I seen him holdin' one of my knives, I knewed right away what he was gonna do with it. I knewed it! So, I says to him, "What you doin' with that? It ain't yours.'"

Mike stopped, his eyes glazed over as the past overtook the present. "'Them's mine! Put it back!' He just laughed at me like I was nothin'. 'You ain't gonna hurt my granny! Don't never think you can!' And he asks me what I intend ta do about it if he don't put it back?"

Mike's frown deepened as the memory continued to play inside his head. "He pushed past me on his way out the door like I weren't even there. Like I weren't nobody. But that weren't the worst part. He had my knife, and I couldn't let him hurt ya. So, I run ahead of him, and I tell him that. He pushes me away ta where I near fell over, tellin' me he ain't gonna hurt nobody, lessen he has ta. I push him back harder. Then he grabs my shirt and pulls me close and says ta me, 'Ya don't know what's at stake. Yer just an ignorant kid. Stay out o' my way'."

Silence fell. The sound of birds chirping and fluttering went unnoticed as two people stood still, waiting. One waited while the next scene came into view, the other for the next part of the story to unfold.

"He done let go o' my shirt," Mike began in a voice so soft his granny was forced to lean forward. "I grabs ahold of 'em and I push so hard he steps backward, but there was somethin' in the way."

"Did he fall, Mike?"

Mike nodded. "He tripped and fell on a corner of the wood I was choppin'. Didn't move. Lay real still. Thought he jist give up. But I was wrong." He looked down at his granny, his face pale but unremorseful. "I dragged him back farther from the road and through the trees. I didn't have no shovel, so I jist covered him with leaves and branches and stuff like that. But, Granny, you don't never need to worry agin. He ain't never gonna hurt you now, Granny."

Mike gently took possession of his granny's arm and they continued. "Not much longer ta go, Granny," he said solicitously. "Then we can sit down a spell if ya need ta."

"I'm quite sure I'll be all right," Miss Treadwell said in a thin voice. She leaned heavily on Mike's arm for support. Her voice shook slightly. Only this time, she wasn't attempting to mimic Mike's granny.

Moments later, they came to a small clearing. Mike stopped short, staring at leaves, dirt, and twigs scattered to the side. His jaw dropped as the color drained from his face. He raced to the spot, fell to his knees, and dug deeper, then shifted to another spot. Finally, he sat back on his heels, staring straight ahead.

Miss Treadwell approached him and gently placed her hand on his shoulder. "Mike," she said softly. "What is it? What's wrong?" She tapped him on the shoulder. "Mike." Slowly, he looked up at her and she repeated her question: "What's wrong?"

"He's gone."

Chapter 36

Ralph heard a voice in his ear. "Karl? What is it? Did you find something?" he said softly.

"Yes. I can see you through the trees, Ralph," Karl said in an equally low voice. "Turn ninety degrees to your left, and you should see me."

Ralph peered through the density of the trees, found Karl, then hurried as quietly as possible to join him. When he reached the spot, he noticed the other officer had donned evidence gloves. When Karl pointed to a stump, Ralph shifted his gaze, and dropped down to inspect the item.

"Mom's camera," Ralph whispered. He slipped on evidence gloves and picked up the camera. He looked through the display panel while his mouth grew increasingly dry. When he looked up, Karl nodded his head.

"You were right, Ralph," Karl said softly. "Your guess was a long shot, but you were right."

Ralph drew the camera strap over his shoulder and looked beyond Karl to the cabin just visible through the trees.

"I saw it, too," Karl said. "Want me to call in the others?" When Ralph nodded, Karl explained where they were relative to the spot they initially entered the woods. The officers should make their way here ASAP. Within minutes, the entire staff of officers gathered around.

"Karl found Miss Treadwell's camera. You can see the outline of a cabin through those trees. She may very well be held prisoner there. All of you know what to do. Let's split up and move forward."

With nods all around, they split into groups of two and headed out. Moments later, Ralph and Karl stood on either side of a window. They pressed their ear against the wall but heard nothing. Edging closer, Ralph peered through the window with one eye then both eyes. When he indicated for Karl to do the same, he whispered, "I see one door, so there's more than one room."

They made their way to the door, tested the handle, and kicked it open. It was empty. Karl crossed the floor to check the bathroom. Ralph's eyes inspected the room finally settling on an object resting on the table. "One of Mom's linen handkerchiefs." Beside the handkerchief was an empty teacup with another empty teacup across from it.

Ralph covered the distance in three strides. Still wearing evidence gloves, he shifted the camera to his other shoulder, and examined the handkerchief more closely. He'd seen all his mother's handkerchiefs, and this was one of them. Where had they taken her?

They circled around the back of the cabin where two officers were stationed. But the focus of their attention wasn't on Ralph.

Ralph followed their gaze. It was his mother's car. He circled the car looking intently through the windows. He tried the driver's side door and it opened. It took several seconds and a great deal of inner strength before he pressed on the button that opened the trunk.

Knowing this would be a traumatic experience for Ralph, Karl stepped quickly to the back of the car while everyone's eyes followed him. Karl peered into the trunk then gave the okay sign to Ralph.

Slowly, Ralph closed the car door and leaned against it for a short time. Collecting himself, he walked up to Jody, who quickly pulled evidence gloves over her hands. "We'll need a car stationed where the cutout is. After you lock this camera in the trunk, drive it to the cutout. Keep it as quiet as you can, then come back here and keep an eye on the cabin. Okay, Jody?"

"Understood." Jody looked over Ralph's shoulder. "That narrow path may lead to the road. It might be the quickest way."

Ralph nodded. "Good thinking, Jody. While you're gone, we'll follow this path back into the woods as far as it goes. Let me know if somebody shows up. Okay?"

"Right," Jody said. "I'll place the camera in the trunk, bring the car to the cutout, and watch the cabin from a protected position. I'll call if someone returns."

"Good," Ralph said.

Once Jody had left, Karl said softly, "You okay?"

"Thanks, Karl. I'll be all right. We need to keep moving." Ralph turned to the others and raised his voice slightly, "Is everything clear?"

When everyone nodded, they spread out and continued back along the path Mike and Miss Treadwell had used a short time before.

Chapter 37

"What do you mean, 'he's gone'?" Miss Treadwell asked, her voice trembling, because she knew exactly what he meant.

Mike transferred his fixated gaze from the scattered debris to his granny. "I thought he were dead, but he weren't. He's somewheres out there. Might be watchin' us right now," he said softly, his eyes slowly tracking across the trees, looking for human movement.

Miss Treadwell's eyes followed Mike's until her knees began to buckle. She was tough for her age, but it had been too much too soon. She took hold of his arm. "I need to sit down."

Mike supported her as she began to crumble and eased her onto the nearest tree stump, where her purse slid off her shoulder and onto the ground. "Soon as you catch your breath, we'd best git back ta the cabin, Granny," he said, his voice quavering while his eyes continued to scan the woods. "That fella might be jist 'bout anywheres, and we don't wanna take no chances."

Miss Treadwell recognized the urgency of their situation. She gathered her purse, rose to her feet, and they made their way in the direction from which they'd come.

It was when they rounded a set of trees that they heard the voice they had both come to dread.

"I wondered how long it would take before curiosity won out," Silky Voice said. He leaned against a tree for support. His face was pale, but his eyes were focused.

Mike pressed his granny behind him. "You tried ta do us a harm, but it didn't work. We don't want no trouble from ya, Mister. There's a bunch of cars jist sittin' 'round back there. Why don't ya take one and leave?"

Silky Voice closed his eyes. "Can't do that, Mike. Wish I could. I really do," he said with that lethally smooth voice of his. "Hadn't intended for it to turn out like this, but now that it has, I have to deal with all the loose ends."

"We ain't no loose ends!"

"It's nothing personal, Mike. But I can't walk away until everything is settled."

"You call keepin' us prisoners and trying to do us a harm not personal?"

Granny tried to step around Mike, but he kept her behind him. "Perhaps I can reason with him, Mike."

"No, Granny. Chocolate candy didn't work, so there's no talkin' him outta this."

"What do you mean 'chocolate candy didn't work'?" Silky Voice said.

"You bought a box o' chocolate candy for us and put poison in it."

Silky Voice shook his head. "I put nothing in the candy I gave you, Mike." His eyes drifted behind Mike to Miss Treadwell. "I apologize. I injected a small amount of insulin in one piece of candy. It was nowhere near enough to really harm you."

"If you didn't mean to do us a harm, then jist let us go," Mike said.

Silky Voice shook his head and pursed his lips as he looked beyond them.

"Looky here," Mike said. "Let Granny go. Me and you can settle this business 'tween us."

"Can't do that, Mike."

"Why?!"

"She's seen me and knows who I am."

Miss Treadwell's brows drew together. She leaned to the side and studied the man with the silky voice. "I have no idea who you are, except a cold-blooded killer. Other than that, I know nothing about you." She swallowed hard, trying to be brave for the sake of the young man shielding her. "Be reasonable. People are looking for us. Looking for me. And despite your best efforts, they'll find me. If they find Mike and me alive and unharmed, it will be much better for all of us."

"But you will know who I am in a very short period of time, Miss Treadwell. That is why I cannot allow you to leave the woods. I deeply regret it, but I have no other choice."

It took several seconds for Miss Treadwell to react to the shock. "You know my name. You know who I am."

"Indeed. I know who you are."

"But how?"

Silky Voice's smile was thin. "I took the liberty of searching through your purse when you were unconscious in the car. I visited you in the hospital. Room 324 if I'm not mistaken."

Silence filled the woods for the next thirty seconds as the two potential victims allowed this to seep through their frozen minds.

"You could have killed me both times. Why didn't you?"

"It was never my intention to kill or even harm you, just to keep you in a state of confusion. The police would come to consider you an unreliable witness." Silky Voice drew his hand across his brow and sighed. "The hospital. Well, I changed my mind and left."

Mike reached behind and gave Granny's hand a squeeze. "You jist do what I tells you to do without no arguments. Do ya hear me, Granny?"

"Mike…."

"On the count o' three, ya run fast as ya can back past that there cabin and down ta the road. Ya got that?"

"Mike, I cannot…."

"One, two…."

Silky Voice rushed forward while Mike pressed his granny in the direction of the main path. She tripped, fell, and lay still while Mike stood his ground, determined to protect her. He grabbed a sturdy branch, using both hands to swing it in front of him, keeping Silky Voice at bay.

Silky Voice hesitated, gauging the swings so he could move in when the limb reached its farthest point away from him.

Suddenly, both men stopped and listened. Crushing leaves was the sound they heard—crushing leaves headed in their direction. And too many leaves to be one person.

Silky Voice disappeared through the trees. This was a setback, but he had developed an alternate plan days ago. It was risky and a last resort he hoped he'd survive.

Ralph and his team of officers crept along, then stopped at the sound of voices. Their pace quickened and soon broke through the trees into a clearing where they found Miss Treadwell sitting on the ground with a young man kneeling beside her, holding her hand.

"He went that way!" Mike shouted, pointing his arm.

"Did you see where he pointed?" When all heads nodded, Ralph said, "Spread out but maintain visual contact with each other." He turned to the officer standing next to him and said, "Jody's near the cabin. I'm going to send her to the cutout. She may need backup in case he heads in that direction." The officer nodded and left. "Stay here, Karl." Ralph knelt on the opposite side of Miss Treadwell while Karl stood guard over Mike. "Are you all right?" he said softly.

Miss Treadwell lifted a trembling hand and touched Ralph's face. "I'll be fine." She laid her other hand on the young man's arm. "This is Mike. He's taken great care of me since I got here."

Ralph's focus shifted to the young man who matched the image on the display panel of his mother's camera. "You took care of her?" he said.

"She's my granny! Course I took care o' her! Always done took care o' her!"

Ralph's brows drew together. "Your granny?"

"Yes, dear," Miss Treadwell said firmly, squeezing Ralph's hand.

"I'm Mike's granny."

Ralph studied Mike, slowly nodded and reached for his phone. "Jody, we found Miss Treadwell and one of the men. Yes, she's fine. The other one escaped before we got here. Right now he's somewhere in the woods, but he may be headed for the road, so I want you to station yourself at the cutout. Your backup is on the way, so be on the lookout for him."

With Ralph on one side and Mike on the other, they drew Miss Treadwell slowly to her feet.

"My purse, dear," Miss Treadwell said weakly.

Ralph reached for it, but Mike was faster. He picked up the purse and slid it through his granny's arm onto her shoulder. He was rewarded with a smile while Ralph observed the scene with puzzled amazement. The two men kept a steady hand under her arms as they walked to the main path with Karl positioned directly behind Mike.

"You okay, Granny?"

"I just need a short rest and a cup of tea."

There was that word again. "Granny". Ralph looked down and met his mother's gaze. She smiled and nodded. Ralph wasn't at all sure how this relationship had evolved, but even after being held prisoner, his mother wasn't in the least threatened by this young man.

Slowly, they made their way to the cabin, settled Miss Treadwell in her chair, then observed Mike boil water for tea as if he hadn't a care in the world. "You fellas want some, too? Got plenty o' tea and milk. Sugar too, if you need it."

While Ralph and Karl continued to stare, Miss Treadwell said, "I think tea for the two of us will be perfect, Mike."

Ralph sat back in his chair, tapping his leg with his fingertips as his mother sipped her way through a cup of tea. With color partially restored to her face, he pulled out his phone. "I want you to look at this photo." When he placed the phone on the table in front of Miss Treadwell, she gasped.

"That's the man with the silky voice. The one who gave me an injection in the car and delivered the chocolate candy," she said. "He tried to kill both of us and would have had you not intervened when you did." When Ralph said nothing, she said, "Who is he?"

"John Calisto."

"John Calisto," Miss Treadwell said softly. "But Ralph. I thought he was the man who was murdered. Are you sure?"

"Positive," Ralph said. "I became suspicious when a piece of your candy contained a small amount of insulin. That's when I called Jeb."

"Jeb," Miss Treadwell said. "Your friend who works at the bank?"

"Right. I broke every rule in the book, but I asked him to check if John Calisto withdrew money from some account recently."

"And Jeb said he had?"

"Yes. He must have run out of money, because two days ago, he made a withdrawal using an ATM card." Ralph's phone vibrated and he answered. "Yes? What?!" He drew his free hand over his forehead as he stood. "Everyone to the cutout. I'll be there ahead of you. Call the ambulance. Help him to the cutout so the EMTs can take care of him."

"What happened?" Karl said.

"They lost contact with the officer who was to provide backup for

Jody. Two officers were detailed to look for him. When they found him, he was only partially conscious. His hat, shirt, and sidearm are missing."

Chapter 38

Ralph helped Miss Treadwell to her feet while Karl took hold of Mike's arm. Within a few minutes, they were at the cutout. The cutout was empty. Jody was missing, as was the police car.

Within seconds, two other officers broke through the trees running towards them, while a third knelt just inside the wooded area.

Trying to catch his breath, the first officer to reach the group said, "It's Jody. She seems all right but can't tell us anything."

"Can she talk?" Ralph said.

The officer leaned over placing his hands on his knees, still breathing hard. "Not really. Can't make out what she's trying to say."

"I need to see her." Ralph ran to the officer kneeling on the ground and dropped down beside him. Jody's breathing seemed normal. He touched her arm. "Jody?"

Jody opened her eyes. "I saw the uniform and thought it was my backup," she said vaguely. "He shoved me aside and I tripped and fell.

I must have hit my head on something; I wasn't prepared, and I should have been."

"Just rest, Jody."

The other officer looked up. "The car is gone."

"I know," Ralph said. He stepped away, punched in a number, and brought Chief Henderson up to date. "Look, we need someone in the air to spot where he's going. Chances are he's headed for the interstate, but we don't know that for sure. Would you authorize air support?" After the Chief agreed to bring in all available resources including air support, the call ended.

When two officers arrived half carrying the officer Calisto had impersonated, they placed him beside Jody.

Ralph assessed the situation, realizing two officers were out of the picture, plus someone needed to stay with the injured until the ambulance arrived. That left himself and four other officers with three cars.

He took his mother aside. "I think you should wait for the ambulance and let them check you out at the emergency room."

"Not on your life, Ralph," his mother said firmly. "I have a very vested interest in this, I'm feeling much better, and I wish to go along. I promise to stay out of the way, but I do want to see this through."

Ralph couldn't sacrifice manpower for someone to see her home and stay with her. In any case, Calisto may very well be waiting for her at the house. To fully protect her, he needed to take her with him.

"Okay, Mom." He turned to the other officers. "Karl, when we hear from the Chief, you take Mike with you and another officer." He turned to the two remaining officers and said, "You take the third car. We'll leave one car here." Everyone's adrenaline was on high alert. "Chief is calling in air support because we have no idea which direction Calisto took." He sighed, and added, "We can't move out till we know where he's headed."

But, in the end, they didn't need air support.

Chapter 39

After clearing up the backlog of work, Sam cleared her desk and said goodbye to Paul. She slowly made her way out the front door to her car but stopped and turned when she heard a car directly behind her. An officer she had never seen got out of the police car and approached her.

"Ralph found Miss Treadwell and she's safe. He needs samples collected and is concerned he'll contaminate the evidence. He's hoping you'll return with me and take care of it."

Sam closed her eyes and sighed with relief. Ralph's mother was safe. After settling in their seats, the police officer left the parking lot at an easy pace.

They headed out of town on the main road in the general direction of the cutout.

"I don't remember seeing you before, and I don't know your name," Sam said.

He hesitated just a fraction of a second. "Jerry. Name's Jerry." He glanced at Sam. "You look tired, Sam. Why don't you lay your head back and rest? I'll let you know when we're nearly there."

Sam's eyes were grainy from lack of sleep, so she didn't internalize the hesitation. She laid her head back and drifted off to sleep.

Ralph's phone vibrated. It was the lab calling. "Sam?" he said.

"No, Ralph. It's Paul. Look. Sam worked the night shift and stuck around to help with the backlog. She's really beat. So if you need help collecting evidence, why don't I come out so Sam can go home and get some sleep?"

Ralph hesitated as he failed to make sense of the underlying message. "Paul, I don't understand what you're talking about."

"Well, I just assumed you needed help. Police car rolled in here not two minutes ago, talked to Sam who was about to leave, and she got in the car with him. I assumed it was because you needed help," Paul said. "But look, you can radio the officer and tell him to bring her back. She can get in her car and go home. Just tell me where you are, and I'll come instead."

Ralph's face drained of color. "Can you tell me what the officer looked like?"

"What did he look like? What do you mean what did he look like?" Paul said.

Ralph pressed his hand against his forehead. "This is important, Paul. Just tell me as much as you can about him."

"Well, he was maybe three or four inches taller than Sam. On the thin side. Mid-thirties at a guess. His hair was brown, what I could see of it," Paul said.

"Did Sam appear to get in the car of her own free will or was she forced into the car?"

"Her own free will?! What's going on here, Ralph?"

"I'm not sure, Paul. That's why I need you to answer the question."

"Well, he talked to her for a few seconds. She seemed relieved about what he said and got in the car with him," Paul said. "Look, Ralph, something's wrong here or you wouldn't be asking these questions. What's going on?"

Ralph hesitated, but he needed Paul's full cooperation. "A police car has been stolen. The man who picked up Sam wasn't an officer."

"You mean Sam's been kidnapped!"

"I don't know for sure, but I need to find out," Ralph said. "Which way did the car turn when it left your parking lot?"

"Kidnapped! You can't be serious, Ralph."

"Paul, which way did he turn?"

"Uh, left. He turned left."

"You sure about that?"

"I'm sure, Ralph. He turned left out of the parking lot."

"Okay. Thanks, Paul."

"Look, Ralph. As soon as you find out anything, you let me know!"

"I will, Paul. I promise," Ralph said, then made another call. "Chief, Sam McKean from the lab may have been kidnapped by John Calisto."

"Kidnapped?! Well, why didn't you…." Chief Henderson paused. He'd been in Ralphs's position a number of times. "Okay, tell me what you know."

"Paul called, said a police car stopped in the lab's parking lot, and she

241

got in the car with him. She didn't appear to be forced. We don't know what he said to get her into the car, but Calisto is armed. He turned left out of the parking lot, which means he may be headed for the main road out of town. Now that he has Sam, he needs to cover as much distance as he can. Even more reason to believe he's headed for the interstate."

"Okay," Chief said. "I already called in air support. Even though we have a good idea where he's headed, we still need to know which way he turns when he gets there."

"Right. We're on our way. We're quite a bit closer to the interstate than he is right now. We should be able to intercept him. It's Sam I'm concerned about."

"I'm concerned about her, too. Keep me posted," Chief Henderson said.

For sixty nerve-racking seconds, Ralph paced, trying to draw up a plan to stop Calisto so nobody got hurt. "What we need is to create a barricade. It has to look like an accident so Calisto is forced to stop without becoming suspicious. It won't look like an accident with four police cars involved, which is all we have available."

"Nope," Mike said. "That ain't true."

"What do you mean?" Ralph said.

"Police cars ain't all you got."

"I know, Mike," Ralph said, but there was a glint in the boy's eyes. "What are you suggesting?"

"I got me an idea."

"What kind of idea?" Ralph said, trying to keep doubt from seeping into his voice.

"Somebody done learned me how ta flip a car," Mike said, with more than a little pride in his voice.

"Flip a car," Ralph murmured.

"Sure! I knows how ta flip a car so it lands pretty much anywheres I want it to."

Ralph stroked his chin. "That might just work. But he'd spot his van in a heartbeat. That only leaves, uh, your grandmother's car, and I don't want to use it."

"Don't have ta," Mike said.

"What do you mean, we don't have to? I thought Calisto took all the keys. That only leaves your grandmother's keys."

"Ya done forgot 'bout that there car belongin' to the fella I used to drive fer. It's way back in the woods. That Calisto fella took the key like I said, but he didn't know nothin' 'bout a spare. It's in the wheel well. Won't take me two seconds to git it."

"But Calisto might recognize it."

"Yep, he sure 'nough would if I flip it so it rests with the top o' the car facin' his way. But I don't plan on doin' that," Mike said. "I plan on flippin' that there car so the bottom of it faces him."

"You know how to do that?"

"I sure enough do."

Even with all the strain that had dominated Ralph's life for the past two weeks, a slow smile crept onto his face for a few seconds. "You know something, Mike? That's brilliant and it just might work."

Chapter 40

Sam awakened, looked out the window, and checked her watch. Nearly twenty minutes had gone by. "Where are we going, Jerry?"

"Ralph is on a side road just north of the Cameron-Bedford County border."

"But I thought the investigation was near the river at the cutout where they found Miss Treadwell," Sam said.

"There's new evidence, so the crime scene has shifted to include this area as well."

Sam nodded, but even with a few minutes' sleep, her mind was more attuned to details as well as subtleties. He appeared calm, but there was an underlying tension about him. Was it the case or something else? In that glance, she noticed something that had escaped her initially. His shirt and hat were standard for a police officer. But his slacks were not. It just didn't fit.

Slowly, a feeling of vulnerability settled over her as she realized she'd met all of the Bedford County Police Officers. Was Jerry newly hired? Or was he something else?

Sam moistened her lips. "Ralph mentioned one of the officers was in the hospital. Phillip? I think it's Phillip. How's he doing? Ralph said he was involved in an accident. Is he out of the hospital?"

Jerry hesitated. "Far as I know, he's fine."

"Good," Sam said. A plan. It had to be something that wouldn't draw attention. She allowed her purse to slide to the floor, reached inside, and felt for the phone. Her last call had been to Ralph. If she pressed the redial button and muted the sound, would Ralph understand what was happening? She left the phone beside her foot and returned her purse to her lap.

Ralph placed his hand on Mike's shoulder. "Okay, Mike," he said, knowing he was taking the greatest risk of his career, which after this, may be short-lived. "We feel certain he's headed for the interstate. What we need to do is get ahead of him."

Mike grasped the situation and understood instinctively what needed to be done. "Ya want me to git ahead of that Calisto fella and flip the car, so it blocks both lanes o' traffic. Trap him so he can't drive past me, right?"

Ralph, along with everyone else, stared admiringly at this young man who developed the initial plan and grasped what needed to be done. "And you said you have the keys to that car we saw about half a mile into the woods, right?"

"Sure do. That fella done took one set. He didn't know I got me a spare hidden in the wheel well," Mike said. "Couldn't move it anyways 'cause he said I'd be picked up in no time."

"Good. Let's get it," Ralph said, nodding to Karl. The three fell into step and made their way rapidly past the cabin, till they arrived at the car with the blood stain in the backseat.

While Mike reached into the wheel well, Karl glanced at Ralph and whispered, "He could just take off if he wanted to."

"I've thought of that. Our only leverage is Miss Treadwell."

Karl's eyebrows rose and fell. "I know, but how long will that delusion last?"

"No idea. I'm more worried that Mike won't be able to flip the car so all Calisto sees is the underside of it. If he can't do that, Calisto will recognize this car and understand what we're doing."

"Maybe," Karl said. "If we're lucky, his mind will be on other things."

"Right. If we're lucky."

"Do you think an officer should go with him?"

Ralph shook his head. "I think he'd better go solo." The phone vibrated in his pocket, and he checked the caller. "It's Sam."

"You said they're gathering evidence somewhere north of the Cameron-Bedford border?" Sam said.

"Right. We'll catch the interstate and take the last exit before we enter Cameron County."

"Okay," Sam said, hoping Ralph heard that. She peered ahead but wasn't sure how far she could take this without creating suspicious.

"We're just passing Weaver's Market so it shouldn't take us more than twenty minutes to get there."

"Hope not."

Ralph muted his phone and continued to monitor, but all was silent on the other end. First his mother, and now Sam. He checked his watch. His face reflected the strain he tried to suppress. The clock continued to tick on their brief window of opportunity. "Let's get the car back to the cutout, Mike."

Mike slid behind the wheel while Ralph sat beside him, and Karl sat in the back. Seconds later, they pulled into the clearing.

"Look, Mike. There'll be two police cars behind you until we get to the main road leading to the interstate. At that point, the two cars behind you will stay on the side road and wait until Calisto passes by. When that happens, they'll both pull out far enough behind him that he doesn't spot them."

"Will you be in one of them there police cars behind me?" Mike said.

"No, I decided we'll take your grandmother's car. I'll be in the lead, and you'll follow me. When we know Calisto is close, you'll flip your car, and I'll turn around. If there's any space open on the road, I'll block it, but it will appear as though I'm trapped on the other side of your car. I don't want you to get hurt, Mike. I have protective gear in the trunk of the police car. I'd like you to wear it."

"I don't need no gear or nothin' like that," Mike said.

Ralph glanced at his mother. She stepped forward and placed her hand on Mike's arm. "Mike, I'd feel so much better if you'd wear the protective gear."

"You worried about me, Granny?"

"Yes, I'm worried."

"Okay," Mike said. "I'll wear it. When do I flip the car?"

"When you hear from me," Ralph said. "What's your cell number?"

"That fella done took my phone and got rid of it. Said it was too risky havin' a phone for very long."

"Karl, we'll need to take a phone from one of the injured officers," Ralph said, then turned to his mother. "We need to use your car. Are your keys in your purse?"

"Of course." Miss Treadwell dug in her purse and handed them over.

Ralph ran back down the path. It took three tries to start it. His hope was it wouldn't fail them at a critical time.

Chapter 41

Miss Treadwell glanced at the passenger side mirror of her car. Mike was behind them followed by the two police cars. "Why did you want to take my car, Ralph?"

"Because once we reach the main road leading to the interstate, the police cars will wait on side roads until Calisto passes by, but we'll still be in front of Mike's car. When he flips the car, I'm going to turn around and face his car as if I'm trapped on the other side. If Calisto sees a police car, he'll know it's a trap. It won't take him long to figure out it's a trap, but I'm trying to buy as many seconds as I can."

"Very clever, Ralph." She fought the temptation to lay her head back because Ralph would realize her strength was rapidly waning. She glanced at her chosen son and realized he wasn't far behind. She knew he was listening for Sam's voice. There had been nothing but silence for the last ten minutes. He hid his anxiety well, but it was obvious to someone who had raised and loved him for twenty-two years.

From their current position, Sam knew they were only fifteen minutes from the interstate. Checking the speedometer, perhaps they'd arrive sooner than that. She tightened her seatbelt. Had Ralph heard her? Did he understand where they were? If he didn't, she wasn't sure what the future held or if there would even be a future.

Suddenly, the silence was broken.

"Look, I—I need your help."

"What do you mean?" Sam said, with a surprisingly steady voice. "What kind of help?"

"I need to…." Calisto swallowed as his brows drew together. "I need to tell you a story, so you'll understand."

"All right. I'm listening."

"My name is John Calisto. I work for the Cameron County DA's office."

The shock reverberated through Sam. "But," she said, the shock resonating in her voice. "I thought you were dead. I thought you were the murder victim."

Calisto glanced at Sam; his eyes widened. "You thought I was the one who was dead? If I'd only known that," he said, shaking his head. "When I spoke to Ralph's brother in the café, he said they had no idea who the victim was."

"You spoke to Teddy? How did you know he was Ralph's brother?"

As perspiration gathered, Calisto drew his hand across his forehead. "I placed a miniature microphone on Miss Treadwell's purse. I needed to know what she'd remember."

"And you just happened to have a miniature microphone with you?"

"Yes, I just happened to have one with me. Has the word gotten around that I'm the supposed victim?"

Suddenly, this was information overload. Sam drew an unsteady breath. "Well, I'm not sure. The Bedford Police, of course. I believe Ralph spoke with the DA's office in Cameron County. I really don't know who else might know."

"The DA's office. Charles Caliban, the DA and his assistant, Mark Jurvic. Do they know?"

Sam stared at Calisto for a moment. "I have no idea. Is it important?"

"Important? I'll tell you in a few days if I'm still around," Calisto said. He closed his eyes and drew a shaky breath.

"Are you all right?" Sam said

Calisto ignored Sam's question. "It wasn't in the newspapers or on the news. Uh, it just reported the possibility of a murder, but there was no mention of a missing person to go with it." He drew his hand across his damp forehead again. "No suspect mentioned either. At least that's what I heard."

"Yes, that's all they would release because they hadn't found the body. And they couldn't really begin to look for the perpetrator of the crime until they found it or gathered evidence that pointed to someone."

John Calisto shook his head. "But what made them think I was the murder victim?"

"A pen," Sam said. "A pen with the words 'Cameron County District Attorney' written on it, so they assumed the person who was killed worked in the DA's office. You were the only person unaccounted for."

"My pen?" Calisto said vaguely, his face glistening with perspiration.

"Oh, yes. I wondered what happened to it."

"Do you know who the murdered victim is?"

"Sure, I know who it is."

"Are you going to tell me?"

When Karl saw the police car carrying John Calisto and Sam McKean fly past where they were waiting on a side road, he called Ralph. "Just spotted them. They're headed your way."

"Is Sam in the car?"

"Yes, Sam is in the car."

"Thanks, Karl," Ralph said, then relayed the message to Mike. "Time for you to flip the car, Mike. You still okay with it?"

"Yep, I can do it," Mike said. Twenty seconds later, the car lay on its side as it slid down the highway, blocking two lanes of traffic.

Miss Treadwell turned and looked anxiously through the back window. "Do you think he'll be all right?" Once the car came to a stop, she said, "Shouldn't we check on him?" But a call came in. It was Mike.

"I'm okay," Mike said, his voice slightly shaken. "Want me to jist stay here?"

"Right, just stay there. Calisto isn't far behind us. Thanks, Mike," Ralph said. He made a U-turn and parked in the only space wide enough for a car to get through.

Calisto shook his head. "Can't tell you who the murder victim is. Not yet."

Sam bit her lip as she looked out the passenger side window. "Did you kill him?"

Calisto closed his eyes briefly. "It was an accident. I know what you're thinking. Everyone says it was an accident, but in this case, it truly was an accident."

This man didn't look like a person capable of murder, whatever a murderer was supposed to look like. In fact, he looked very ill. His face was pale and glistened with sweat.

"Look, John, I can't possibly do anything to help you. Just pull over and I'll get out."

"I can't do that, Sam. I'm not going to hurt you. I just need some insurance right now," John said. "Look, I need to use your phone. Okay?"

Sam glanced at the speedometer again. Eighty-five. She dragged her eyes away as she realized the phone was on the floor. She'd have to retrieve it without arousing suspicion. She briefly searched through her purse, then looked on the floor. "Must have slipped out. Uh, do you want me to get the number for you?"

Calisto paused while he considered the lesser of two evils. "No, just give me the phone."

For a split second, Sam considered calling Ralph, but she didn't want to be trapped in a car with someone who had little to lose. She handed him the phone.

Calisto's eyes tracked up and down as he punched in two numbers at a time. His hand shook as he slowly drew it to his ear.

"I need help," Calisto said weakly. He listened for a moment, and said, "Look, I'll either be at the Bedford Police Station, the hospital, or…." He closed his eyes briefly. "Or at the city morgue. Yes, as soon as you can." His hand dropped and the phone slid onto the floor at his feet.

Sam studied the face of a man who had collapsed even though his hands were still on the wheel and his unfocused eyes stared out the windshield. "You're ill," she said. "You need medical attention. Let me call an ambulance." When Calisto didn't respond, she said, "When is the last time you took your insulin?" Still no response.

"It's a trap," Calisto said, staring ahead with half-closed eyes.

Sam transferred her focus from Calisto to the car ahead turned on its side. "There's been an accident."

"No, it's intended for me," Calisto whispered. John Calisto's left hand slid from the steering wheel, then his right hand. His head fell back on the headrest, but his foot was still on the accelerator.

Sam unbuckled her seatbelt, shoved his foot aside, and pressed on the brake. When they came to a stop, she searched the floor for her phone, and dialed the emergency number.

Chapter 42

Ralph and Chief Henderson sat across the table from Mike in the interrogation room at the Bedford Police Station. Mike stared at his folded arms with his mouth firmly shut.

Ralph studied the young man who refused to answer any questions, much less make eye contact. Remembering the tea session in the cabin, he said, "Would you like some tea, Mike?"

Mike looked up. "Sure. I'd like some tea. But I need ta see Granny first. Make sure she's okay and stuff."

"She's tired and needs to rest Mike."

"Now, looky here. I ain't sayin' 'nothin' till I see Granny! And I got a whole lot to tell ya!"

Ralph sat back in his chair. Trumped by a teenager. He looked at Chief Henderson, who nodded. "Okay, let's go." They headed to the lunchroom where his mother and Sam were seated at a table.

"Do you know how to make tea?" Ralph asked the nearest officer.

When the officer looked slightly puzzled, Sam stood and announced that she'd handle it.

Mike sat next to his granny, searching her face for signs of fatigue. "Yer looking awful tired, Granny. They treatin' ya good?"

"Yes, I'm fine, Mike. Are you all right?"

"I'm okay, Granny. Jist worried about ya is all."

Ralph cleared his throat and turned to his mother. "Mike has information vital to the case. He'd feel more comfortable in your presence."

"Of course. Shall we stay here or walk down the hall to one of those dreary rooms you use to interrogate people?"

Ralph knew without a doubt that he'd lost total control of this interview. But the goal was to find the car and the body. "We'll stay here," he said, then added with as much equilibrium as possible. "And drink our tea." He nodded to a police officer who set up the equipment to tape the interview.

Miss Treadwell placed her hand on Mike's arm. "Tell me what you know, Mike."

"See, it's like this, Granny. These here folks want ta know where I done put everythin', but I thought, you know, I should run it past ya first."

"Very sensible, Mike. Now, start from the beginning."

Mike clasped Granny's hand. "I picked up that there fella at the garage in Cameron same as I always do. He don't give me no address just tells me where ta turn and stuff. I knowed pretty quick where we was headed, 'cause I just come from there. He don't say nothin' the whole way there, 'cept ta give me directions and tell me ta pull over beside that there crick. And 'member, Granny, he says ta me I was ta stay put no matter what?"

"Yes, Mike. I remember that."

"He walks a ways and 'round some bushes, then I heared voices gettin' louder and louder. And I heared this sorta poppin' sound. After that, I don't hear nothin'. Pretty soon, this guy comes runnin' ta me with blood all over him."

"Was it the same man you drove to Muddy Creek or someone else?" Ralph said.

"It were someone else. I jist found out his name today. It's that there John Calisto fella. The fella I drove here is dead."

"Calisto didn't give you his name?" Ralph said.

"Nope. I jist called him Mister. Same thing I called that other fella what was dead by now."

"Was John Calisto injured, or do you think it was the other man's blood?" Ralph said.

"John Calisto weren't hurt. The blood belong ta the other fella."

Ralph studied Mike, and said softly, "Who was the other man, Mike? The man you worked for?"

"The other guy? Don't know. Never told me."

Ralph leaned forward in his chair. "You have no idea who he was?"

"Nope. Said I didn't have ta worry none 'bout my health' if I didn't knowed who he was. So I never asked one more time."

Ralph wondered if the popping sound could have been a gun with a silencer attached to it, but he didn't want to suggest something he'd be held accountable for in court. He stifled a sigh and signaled to his mother.

"What happened next, Mike?" she said.

"I takes that John Calisto fella back ta the cabin 'cause he wants ta clean up. Then he says we need ta go back and hide that there body and car afore anybody finds it or I'll be next."

"Are you sure he said that, Mike?" Ralph said. "'We need to go back and hide that body and car before anybody finds it or I'll be next'."

"Sure, I'm sure. That's what he says, awright. 'I'll be next if we don't hide everythin'.' Says there's some kind of informant or something where he works, and he can't take no chances."

"Informant," Ralph said. "Did he name anyone? I mean did he tell you where he worked or who the informant was?"

"I done asked, but he wouldn't say nothin' 'bout it." Mike turned remorseful eyes to his grandmother.. "I'm sure sorry ta tell you this, Granny, but when we got there and seen you, that fella runs you off the road and gives you a shot in the arm ta knock ya out."

"I know, Mike," his granny said. Had he completely forgotten he'd already told her this? "But I'm all right. Now, what happened after that?"

"Well." Mike blinked as his mind drifted back to that day. "We leave Granny and drive back ta that there crick. He drops me off where his car and, uh, the body is, and tells me ta clean up stuff 'cause he's got ta take some new pictures with yer camera."

Ralph and Miss Treadwell exchanged glances.

"But, Mike," Ralph said. "He took the card out of Miss Treadwell's camera. Where did he get another digital card?"

"He had a camera with him. He done switched the card in his own camera with Granny's card. He had all kinds o' stuff packed in that there car o' his. He grabbed a bunch of stuff out o' the trunk and puts it in that there other fella's car. Jist said ta put the body in his car and hide it somewheres, 'cause everybody'd be lookin' for his car."

Ralph leaned in. "Is the digital card still in Calisto's camera?"

"Sure is. Didn't take it out or nothin', so it's still there."

"Okay," Ralph said. "Let me get this straight. The man you drove to Muddy Creek left his car, walked to the other side of the bushes to John Calisto's car, and that's where the murder took place." When Mike nodded, Ralph continued, "You took Calisto to the cabin, where he cleaned up, and returned to the scene of the murder. Calisto took whatever he needed out of his car and transferred it to your employer's car. He switched digital cards, then you put the body in Calisto's car and hid it somewhere. Is that right?"

"Yep, that's right."

"And the body is still in John Calisto's car. Right?"

"Yep, that's where it is."

Ralph nodded at his mother.

"Mike, where did you take the car with the body inside?"

For the first time since Miss Treadwell met the young man, he smiled. "People think I'm stupid, but I'm not. I 'membered a junkyard a few miles down the road. There's bunches o' ole cars just sittin' there any which way. I drives it in there clear ta the back and hides it behind some other ones. I figure nobody'd think ta look for a car in a junkyard. Then I walks back."

"Mike," Ralph said gently. "Would you be willing to show us exactly where the car is?"

When Miss Treadwell nodded, Mike said, "Okay. I'll takes ya there." He took his granny's hand again. "You stay here and rest, Granny. I don't want ya seein' the likes of that. I got ta show these here fellas somethin', then I'll be right back. Okay?" He rose, patted her arm, and joined Jody and another officer down the hallway.

"Do you want to go home?" Ralph said softly.

Miss Treadwell thought for a moment. "No, I'd rather wait here till you get back. I'll just lie down on the cot for a while." Ralph got up to leave but his mother called him back. "Ralph, what is going to happen to Mike?"

Ralph sat down again and reached for his mother's hand. "Mike will be evaluated. Probably in a hospital. He may have to remain there for a while until a diagnosis is made and they decide on a course of treatment."

"I need to visit him, Ralph."

"I know. Don't worry, Mom. I'll see to that. Mike will need your support." Ralph kissed his mother on the top of her head then caught up with the officer and Mike as they headed out the backdoor.

Chapter 43

Three vehicles drove along Muddy Creek. The lead car carried Mike and two other officers. Sam, who insisted on joining Paul from the lab, followed behind the lead car. Ralph drove independently, so he could leave for the hospital once he was sure Mike really was taking them to the location of the car and body.

"Here," Mike said to Jody. "Turn in right here."

They drove through the junkyard where cars, trucks and motorcycles waited to have their parts stripped from them.

As they neared the end, Mike said, "There. Last car."

Jody stopped significantly ahead of that area to give them room to search. Everyone walked between stripped cars and approached Calisto's car from the back. There was nothing significant about it except the foul odor. It looked like the car any moderately successful attorney would drive.

Ralph donned evidence gloves, clothing, and mask. Once the trunk was opened, everyone could see the body which had laid there for two weeks.

It was a young man with dark brown hair, medium build and well dressed, just as Miss Treadwell had described. But what she hadn't seen was the gun. There was a gun with a silencer attached to the end of it.

Ralph's eyes searched the trunk, then stopped when he found the camera. He lifted it carefully out of the trunk and stepped away. Opening the display panel, he inspected the photos. He saw all the shots his mother had taken that day. Closing his eyes, he felt the sting of guilt at having doubted her. He signaled for Sam. When she reached his side, he said, "All the photos Mom took are on here. Would you take care of this, Sam?"

Sam studied his face as she took possession of the camera. "I'll see to it, Ralph. Do you need to leave?"

"Yes, I need to see if Calisto is well enough to tell us anything. I'll check back later."

He called Karl in transit. Calisto was stable and had been transferred to a hospital room on the third floor. Karl and another officer were stationed outside Calisto's room. Perhaps he'd be permitted to talk to him for a short time.

Ralph spoke briefly to Karl and another officer outside John Calisto's room before passing through the doorway with Karl following behind him. The nurse who had taken care of his mother weeks earlier had just finished checking the IV portal. "Is it all right if we ask John Calisto a few questions?"

Ms. Franklin smiled and nodded. "I'll return in five minutes to check on him," she said softly. "How's your mother? She was in a room down the hall from here as I remember."

"Yes, she was. She's doing fine," Ralph said. "Thanks for asking."

After checking her watch, Ms. Franklin left Room 368.

"We need to keep this short, Calisto. What can you tell us?" Ralph said.

Calisto moistened his lips as he organized his thoughts. "I'd been working on organized crime cases off and on for a couple of years," he said. "As new information came in, I'd drop what I was doing and return to the case, but it was always a dead end. Tracks professionally covered up. That's when I suspected an informant was in the DA's office. It was the only answer. Then came my first real break."

"Estelle Lucca," Ralph said.

Calisto glanced at Ralph. "How did you find out about Estelle?"

"Phone call. Unidentified source. Go on."

"I often ate at a restaurant after work. One night, the waiter delivered a note in a sealed envelope. It was from Estelle. Never met her," Calisto said, closing his eyes for a moment. "I knew very little about her except she was related to the Lucca family, but not part of the business, if you understand what I mean."

"I understand," Ralph said. "Estelle wasn't mixed up in organized crime."

"Right," Calisto said. "She asked me to meet her at a small café in another town the following evening. I knew of Antonio Lucca. He'd slid under the radar screen for a number of years. One of those expertly covered up tracks I mentioned."

When Calisto hesitated, Ralph said, "So you met her?"

"Yeah, I met her. Estelle's father and Antonio's father are cousins. The entire Lucca family met every year. Must have been over thirty of them. Then one year, something happened."

"What was that?" Ralph said.

"Antonio became interested in Estelle. He asked her out. Mario, Estelle's father, had never told her about the family business. Estelle just looked at Antonio as a distant cousin. But he did something stupid," Calisto said, drawing a shallow breath. "Antonio tried to impress her. He gave her a few details about his role in the family business. A friend of hers works in the DA's office. She wouldn't tell me who it was. This friend knew I worked on cases involving organized crime. The next day Estelle sent me the note. Not long after that, I discovered something."

When Calisto hesitated, Ralph said, "What did you discover?"

"My hunch was right. There actually was an informant inside the DA's office. That's why people were slipping under the radar. I just didn't know which one it was. Someone very high up."

"You still don't know who it is?" Ralph said.

Calisto shook his head. "One of two people. Either Mark Jurvic, assistant to the DA, or the DA himself, Charles Caliban."

"How did you narrow the informant down to those two?" Ralph said.

"I recruited an informant inside the Lucca family. Even though I paid him, he was still putting his life on the line." Calisto grew quiet.

"What happened to him?" Ralph said.

"You know what happened. He disappeared. Only two people knew about this guy."

"Caliban and Jurvic."

"Right. Caliban and Jurvic. Look, if I could gather enough evidence to prosecute the Lucca family, I needed to record what Antonio was telling Estelle. While I was at it, maybe Antonio would reveal whether Caliban or Jurvic was the traitor in the DA's office." Calisto took another shallow breath. "I gave her a miniature microphone to attach to her purse. After that, I had a record of everything he said for several weeks. By the time the guy informing on the Lucca family disappeared, Caliban and Jurvic knew about Antonio and Estelle. They knew about the recording. When the informant I was paying to spy on the Lucca family disappeared, I knew Estelle and I may be next."

"You're a lawyer. You know recording conversations may not be admissible in court."

"I knew that. I hoped Antonio would give me something to go on so I'd know what direction to take. What line of investigation to pursue."

"Okay," Ralph said. "Did Antonio mention who the leak was in the DA's office?"

"No, never mentioned who it was. Maybe too frightened of what would happen if he leaked that kind of information to Estelle."

Ralph checked his watch. Two minutes to go. "What then?"

"After Estelle was killed, I had to get away. Someone called telling me he had information about who ordered the hit-and-run. I still had my phone with me. I agreed to meet him." Calisto closed his eyes for a second. "It surprised me the meeting place was close to where I'd taken the van. I was stupid. Well, I was still in a state of shock over Estelle. After that, I realized I was definitely on their hit list, so I went into hiding."

"Okay," Ralph said. "I need to talk about my interview with Mike. He took us to the junkyard where he hid your car. We found a gun with the body. Who was it, John?"

"So that's where he took my car," John said. "It was Antonio Lucca."

Ralph and Karl exchanged glances. "But I thought Antonio Lucca was out of the country."

John attempted a sour laugh but coughed instead. "That's what they wanted everyone to believe."

"There was a gun with the body."

John closed his eyes. "When I met Antonio along Muddy Creek that day, he blamed me for Estelle's death. Said if I hadn't recorded their conversations, she'd still be alive. We argued, and Antonio pulled the gun from his shoulder holster. We fought and the gun went off. The gun never left Antonio's hand." He opened his eyes and looked at Ralph. "You know what's so utterly ridiculous about what he said?"

"Tell me."

"When the informant in the DA's office found out Antonio was spilling information to Estelle, he ordered the hit-and-run," John said. "And as a lesson, he ordered Antonio to execute it."

Ralph hesitated. "Antonio was the hit-and-run driver?"

John nodded. "He told me that it was either his life or Estelle's."

The door to the room opened and Ms. Franklin stepped in. Ralph placed his hand on John Calisto's shoulder. "Thanks, John. Rest and get better."

"Ralph," John whispered. When Ralph turned, he said, "I came to the hospital when your mother was here. I would never hurt her. I only wanted to keep her confused. I needed time to hide and sort things out. But I couldn't do it, so I left."

Ralph stepped to the side of the bed. "I don't understand…."

"I'm sorry, officers. The patient needs to rest now," Ms. Franklin said firmly.

Ralph followed Karl out of the room, unable to interpret what John meant by his last statement. In the hallway, the two men joined the other officer. "I've got to check back at the station and take Mom home," Ralph said. "I'll send two others here to relieve you later on."

As the elevator descended to the ground floor, Ralph leaned his head back against the wall. What had John Calisto meant when he said he couldn't do it when he visited Mom in the hospital? Couldn't do what? But as the elevator doors opened on the ground floor, his mind put the pieces together. He understood what John couldn't do.

It had been a long day and Ralph was ready for a break, but that wouldn't happen for hours yet. As he pressed through the front door, Mario and Sophia Lucca were twenty feet away, walking rapidly in his direction.

Ralph stepped back through the door and waited for them. They seemed surprised to see him but stopped immediately and posed a question.

"How's John?" Sophia said, her face anxious and drawn.

Chapter 44

Ralph's brows rose then drew together. The transition from having no idea who Estelle's boyfriend was to asking about John took a moment to adjust. "He's stable. John was running short of insulin so took half doses."

"I told him this would happen," Sophia said.

They seemed unaware of how much this sudden shift had affected him. "The nurse let us interview John for five minutes, but he needed to rest. I doubt if they'll let you into his room just yet. Look, I'd like to talk to you about this. The Visitors Waiting Room is on the other side of the Information Desk. Let's go in there and we can talk for a few minutes." Without waiting to see if they'd accept or refuse his suggestion, he led the way.

Ralph indicated two seats, so the couple faced the light from the hallway. He sat across from them in the shadow. "When I interviewed you at your house, I got the very distinct impression you knew nothing about John Calisto. Obviously that's not the case. What can you tell me about him?"

They were silent as they collected their thoughts. "We didn't know John until three months ago," Mr. Lucca said.

"What happened three months ago?"

"Well, I mentioned that we gathered with the rest of the Lucca family every year. Some were involved in what they called the family business, but most of us were not. We just had regular jobs. The last time we met, Antonio took a liking to Estelle," Mr. Lucca said, giving Ralph a knowing look. "Took her out to dinner a few times, then started showing more romantic interest in her."

"We didn't like it," Mrs. Lucca said. "But Estelle told us they were just friends. That's what she said, but Mario and I knew better."

"What do you mean?" Ralph said.

"Well," Mrs. Lucca hesitated. "He had that look in his eyes. If you know what I mean."

"I understand," Ralph said. "Go on."

"Antonio was stupid," Mr. Lucca said. "He started bragging to Estelle about all the stuff he was doing for the family business and getting away with it."

"What was he doing?"

"Extortion!" Mr. Lucca said. "He claimed he had a territory in some other city. Wouldn't tell her which one, but it was his job to be the heavy. He'd only talk to small businesses where the owners were on the premises. If the owner didn't pay up, either the property got hurt or the owner did."

"Estelle didn't say anything, just listened to him," Mrs. Lucca said. "She told us about it later. She stormed around the room! Furious! Said Antonio couldn't go around terrorizing people like that. She was related to a crook and was going to do something about it!" She shook her head as tears formed in her eyes. "She terrified us. We didn't know what to do. She was young and naïve and didn't understand what could happen."

As before they leaned into each other, gathering comfort from their shared grief.

Ralph gave them a moment. "Tell me how she met John Calisto," he said softly.

Mr. Lucca dabbed his eyes. "A friend of hers works in Personnel at the DA's office. Estelle confided in her and somehow this woman knew John was working on organized crime cases. Told her where John often ate dinner after work. We tried to talk Estelle out of it, but she wrote John a note and they met."

"Do you know who the person in Personnel was?"

The couple looked at each other, but it was too late to hold back now. "Her name is Carol. That's all we know about her except she's lived here for about a year. Moved here from Canada."

Carol. The woman he'd spoken to in Personnel when he first called the DA's office. The same woman who called him giving him information. That's why he recognized her voice. Why hadn't she changed her phone because it was still a Canadian phone number?

"And John agreed to work with Estelle?"

"Yes," Mrs. Lucca said. "They'd have dinner at small places out of town. John talked to her about recording conversations with

Antonio. We couldn't talk her out of that either. He gave her one of those miniature microphones you can attach anywhere, and John would listen and record their conversations."

It all fit together. He attached the same microphone to Mom's purse. "Do you think the hit-and-run was planned?"

"Yes!" Mr. Lucca said. "Someone had to inform Antonio that Estelle was recording their conversations."

"So, someone in the DA's office was the informant. Is that what you're saying?"

"Yes, that's what we're saying," Mrs. Lucca said. "We don't know who it is. Estelle wouldn't tell us. Well, maybe she didn't know either."

"I'm assuming John was the man Estelle followed to Bedford County. Is that right?"

Mr. Lucca nodded. "By then, he felt sure there was an informant in the DA's office, and it may not be safe for either one of them. He thought he may have to ditch his car and phone and hide out somewhere. That was the reason he moved the van up there. He'd convinced Estelle to do the same, and she was making plans to do that. She wanted us to go with her. But I don't know. We're getting up there a bit. Maybe we're too old to hide."

"How did John know about the cabin where he parked his van? Did he know Mike?"

"Oh, let me think," Mr. Lucca said. "I remember now. Antonio mentioned to Estelle that his driver had a little cabin in the woods in Bedford County. Secluded. I don't know anything beyond that. I don't know how he found it. I just know Antonio mentioned the cabin."

"Okay. Pick up where you left off."

Mrs. Lucca took a moment to pick up the thread of the conversation. "We wanted Estelle to leave," Mrs. Lucca said. "And she was going to only…."

Ralph gave them another moment to collect themselves. "Did John call you the night of the hit-and-run?"

Mrs. Lucca shook her head. "Not until very early the following morning. We already knew. The police had come by and told us. We didn't know where he was." She looked at her hands. "She told him not to forget his promise."

"And what promise was that?"

"To continue with the case. Not to give up no matter what happened."

While quietly contemplating John's promise, they overheard a man's voice at the Information Desk.

"Would you give me the room number of John Calisto?"

Chapter 45

When the man walked past the door, Mr. Lucca whispered, "It's Mark Jurvic. Right, Sophia? It's Mark Jurvic, the man who came to interview us that day."

"Yes. But what's he doing here?" Mrs. Lucca said.

Ralph wasn't sure what the assistant to the district attorney was doing here either, but at a guess, it wasn't to wish John Calisto a speedy recovery. "Wait here," he said softly. He was fifteen feet behind Mark Jurvic when he called ahead, "Jurvic!" When there was no response, Ralph moved forward and called his name again. Still there was no response.

They reached the elevator at the same time and Ralph tried the same tactic, knowing the end result. "I thought I'd met you somewhere before. Seemed like your name was Jurvic."

The man eyed him briefly and looked up to see where the elevator was. It appeared to be stuck on the fifth floor. "No, my name is not

Jurvic, and I don't recall meeting you before."

"I see. My mistake," Ralph said. "It's always a little depressing visiting family in the hospital, don't you think?"

"Not visiting family. Just someone who works for me in my office."

"I see," Ralph said again. Except this time, he recognized the voice. He reached for his phone and headed for the Information Desk while he carried on a conversation with the nonexistent caller.

Ralph presented his ID badge, allowing the woman at the Information Desk to view it. "I need to speak to Ms. Franklin, the head nurse, on the third floor immediately," he said.

The woman punched in a number and handed the phone to him. "Ms. Franklin? This is Lieutenant Davies. I have two men stationed outside John Calisto's room. Calisto's life may be in danger. I want you to do exactly what I tell you, and I want you to do it now."

Having completed that call, Ralph stepped away from the Information Desk and spoke with Karl stationed outside Calisto's room. "Is Ms. Franklin coming towards you?" When Karl assured him she was, Ralph said, "A man just entered the elevator on the main floor. He's headed your way. I won't be far behind him. This is what we're going to do."

After Ralph ended the call, he walked rapidly to the elevator and pressed the button to the second floor. When he arrived on the second floor, he took the stairway to the third floor, opened the hallway door a few inches, and watched the man he'd just spoken to walk down the hall towards Calisto's room.

The man checked room numbers even though it wasn't necessary.

There was a man standing beside a door who couldn't be mistaken for anything but a police officer. "My employee is in this room. I'd like to visit him."

The officer nodded to the nurse's station down the hallway. "Have to clear it with them, sir."

Agreeing to the nurse's five-minute rule, he headed back and pressed through the door, making sure it swung shut behind him. "Hello, John," he said, walking briskly to the side of the bed.

John opened his eyes. "How did you know I was here?" he said weakly.

"Does it matter?"

"Of course it matters. I called Mr. and Mrs. Lucca and that was all," John said, his mind sifting through the possibilities. "I know what happened. I could only remember their landline number and you tapped their phone, didn't you, Charles?"

He shrugged. "Again, does it matter?"

"Why are you here?" John said, his voice just barely above a whisper. "No, let me guess. I've become too great a liability, right?"

"Something like that. Nothing personal, John."

John smiled. He'd used words similar to that not long ago. What was Mike's response? "You call trying to do me a harm not personal?"

Caliban's brows drew together at John's odd turn of phrase. He reached inside an inner pocket and withdrew a syringe. "Sorry, John."

"It must have been a shock to find out I wasn't the murder victim. Right? Had to decide what to do about it, didn't you?"

"Yes, it was very inconvenient, John. But at least we know what happened to Antonio. In any case, he couldn't be trusted."

"You know what's kept me going since the night you ordered Estelle's murder?"

"What's kept you going, John?" Caliban said as he inspected the syringe.

John inhaled a shallow breath, and another before responding. "The thought that someday I'd be on the witness stand testifying against you."

"Sorry to disappoint you, John, but that isn't going to happen."

John swallowed and tried to lift himself off the bed but fell back. "I have an impressive list of charges to be filed. I was just waiting to see who the informant was, you or Mark."

"Yes, well, that's why I'm here. To make sure that doesn't happen." He plunged the needle into the IV port. "Just a little extra insulin to send you on your way, John." When John reached for the call button, Charles moved it just out of reach, turned on his heel, and walked rapidly out the door. Once he reached the hallway, he nodded at the police officer, and caught the elevator to the ground floor.

Charles Caliban frowned as he saw the man who had referred to him as "Jurvic" standing near the front door. He ignored him and attempted to pass, but the man blocked his way.

"How was your employee?" Ralph said as Caliban approached the exit.

"Improving," Caliban said, attempting to bypass the man standing in his way.

"He was fine when you left him?" Ralph said.

Caliban stopped. It was his tone of voice rather than the words he used. "Of course he was fine when I left him."

"Good. There's someone who'd like to speak to you in the Visitors Waiting Room," Ralph said, nodding his head to the right.

Caliban glanced at the room, saw no one, and again attempted to move forward. "I don't have time for this."

"Won't take a moment," Ralph said, extending his arm, inviting him to lead the way.

Caliban looked at his watch, then over Ralph's shoulder. Finally, he said, "All right, one minute. That's all the time I can spare." Once inside the door, he spotted Mr. and Mrs. Lucca. He spun around, but Ralph had already closed the door.

"You told us your name was Mark Jurvic," Mr. Lucca said, his voice shaking.

"Were you the one?" Mrs. Lucca said. "Were you the one who ordered Estelle killed? I need to know." When Caliban refused to make eye contact, she said, "John was right. He knew the informant had to be the DA or his assistant. It's you, isn't it?" she said, her voice rising.

Mr. Lucca placed his arm around his wife and drew her face to his shoulder as the tears silently slid down her face.

Charles Caliban's hand shook as he pulled down the sleeves on his suit coat. "I haven't the faintest idea who these people are or what they're talking about."

"That's interesting," Ralph said. "Especially since they seem to know who you are."

"They're mistaken. My name is not Mark Jurvic."

"I know," Ralph said. "It's Charles Caliban, District Attorney for

Cameron County."

Caliban swallowed hard but maintained an outward appearance of calm. "Who are you?" he demanded.

"Lieutenant Davies, Bedford Police."

Caliban's eyes dropped for moment as his sharp attorney's mind weighed his options. Finally, his eyes lifted, and he turned to face Ralph. "I know my rights."

Ralph smiled wryly. "So do I."

Chapter 46

Caliban's hand slipped inside an inner pocket of his suit coat.

"I wouldn't do that if I were you."

Caliban lifted an arrogant eyebrow. "Do what? I haven't the faintest idea what you're talking about."

"I assumed you were reaching for the syringe," Ralph said. "Haven't had an opportunity to get rid of it yet, have you?"

"I'm afraid your meaning eludes me, Lieutenant," Caliban said, using his courtroom voice.

"You saw one officer standing outside John Calisto's room. The other officer was observing your activities through the crack in the bathroom door. He recorded what you said and what John Calisto's response was." Ralph hesitated for effect. "And he saw you inject something into the IV port. You see, I recognized your voice, Mr. Caliban. I also took precautions that my witness wouldn't be harmed. I knew you wouldn't use physical violence, so your options were limited. I asked the nurse to disconnect the IV."

Charles Caliban's eyes widened, but only slightly. He was accustomed to reacting under extreme pressure. "Very interesting story, Lieutenant. But are you charging me?"

"Not yet. I'm waiting for a report from the lab. Then I'll arrest you."

Charles Caliban drew himself to his full height. "In that case, you have no legal right to detain me. I will leave immediately. I have business to attend to." He walked out the door with Ralph close behind but stopped short as he saw a police car waiting outside the front door. He wheeled around. "What is this?"

"Just making sure we don't lose track of you, Mr. Caliban," Ralph said.

"You intend to have me followed?"

Ralph matched his steely gaze. "I do until the lab reports what was in the syringe."

Caliban's eyes dropped. He searched for an escape route but found none. "I wish to consult my attorney."

"I'm sure you do."

Both men and the woman behind the Information Desk turned as a disagreement arose inside the Visitors Waiting Room. The words were garbled, but Mario Lucca's voice was resolute, while there was fear and desperation in the voice of Sophia Lucca.

The Visitors Waiting Room door opened and crashed against the inside wall. Mr. Lucca staggered through with a raised gun in his trembling hand. The look in his eyes was a combination of overwhelming grief and fury.

Ralph stepped forward, raising his hand. "Mr. Lucca, I hope you want justice rather than revenge. I think that's what your wife and John Calisto want. That's what Estelle would want."

"Justice?" Mr. Lucca said. His voice quavered, but his eyes were focused on Charles Caliban. "This will go on for years and years! You call that justice? He's the one who killed Estelle or ordered her killed!"

Mrs. Lucca stood in the doorway, her face white. She took one step forward, her hand still touching the doorframe for support. "Mario," she said weakly. "Don't do this." But Mario's ears were closed to everything except the voice inside his head. Step by step she reached his side and placed her hand on the arm that held the gun. "Don't do this. Am I to lose everything?"

"Sophia, don't you see? I have to do it!"

"I understand how you feel, Mario. But think of us. Is this what Estelle would want? Would she want us to be separated forever?" Sophia pleaded, her eyes searching the side of his face as her husband remained focused on the man responsible for his only child's death.

Ralph stepped back. The only person who could prevent this from happening was the woman standing beside Mario Lucca.

Mario looked down at his wife. "Don't you see, Sophia? The Lucca family will buy the best lawyers in the country to keep Caliban quiet. The case will go on forever. He may even walk out a free man because there won't be enough evidence to convict him. Can't you see that?"

"Yes, I see that. He may walk free. But if you do this, you'll be alone and so will I."

Mario dropped his head and slowly lowered his gun.

Ralph quietly stepped forward. It was over. He placed his hand on Mr. Lucca's shoulder, and gently took the gun away. "Charles Caliban will be convicted. I guarantee it," he said, even though he shared Mario Lucca's concerns.

March 20, 1996

Having attended to the preliminaries, the judge turned to the acting prosecutor and said, "Prosecution, you may call your first witness."

Mark Jurvic rose from his chair. "Thank you, Your Honor. I call to the stand John Calisto."

Before rising from his chair behind the bar, John glanced first at Ralph Davies seated on his right. He sought and squeezed Sophia Lucca's hand to his left. He stood, took one step past Sophia, shook Mario Lucca's hand, smiled at Cynthia Treadwell and Sam McKean seated behind them, and walked to the witness stand.

The bailiff asked the question repeated down through the centuries: "Do you swear to tell the truth, the whole truth, and nothing but the truth?"

John Calisto locked eyes with Charles Caliban, the man who had injected enough insulin into his IV port to kill him, and said, "I do."

~The End~

Made in United States
North Haven, CT
10 December 2022